Anonymous

The Hallow Isle Tragedy

Vol. 1

Anonymous

The Hallow Isle Tragedy
Vol. 1

ISBN/EAN: 9783337409548

Printed in Europe, USA, Canada, Australia, Japan

Cover: Foto ©Andreas Hilbeck / pixelio.de

More available books at **www.hansebooks.com**

THE

HALLOW ISLE TRAGEDY

IN THREE VOLUMES.

VOL. 1.

LONDON:

CHAPMAN AND HALL, 193, PICCADILLY.

MDCCCLX.

CONTENTS OF VOL. I.

HALLOW ISLE TRAGEDY.

CHAPTER I.

TOO LATE FOR THE COACH.

Most of our readers, the very juvenile excepted, must still have a tolerably fresh recollection of the extraordinary movement which, commencing with Church extension in a crusade against the voluntaries, led to division among the Scottish clergy themselves (partly, it would seem, by imbuing them with a taste for some of their voluntary neighbours' opinions), gave

a shake to patronage, and brought on the
famous non-intrusion war, and eventually
met its apotheosis at Auchterarder and
Strathbogie in the defeat of the Church
and the retreat of the dominant party.

The retreat, which, it must be owned,
embraced a large proportion of the talent,
and, it was said at the time, nearly all the
sincerity and piety in the Church (though
there might be some exaggeration here),
was conducted on the rigid old covenant-
ing model.   Their ancient incubus, the
carnal government, was thrown off once
more, under protest, however, of a new
and ingenious tenet professing to demon-
strate the right to State pay without State
interference.   The battle was lost, but the
tenet was set up; and full, apparently, of
confidence in the new world they were
bound for, the devoted adventurers for
conscience' sake left the old world of

kirk and manse, taking with them "*the keys.*"

What a picture was that old spiritual world shut up at the disruption! The Residuaries, as the remnant was termed who refused to come out of the shattered and blackened ruin, half ashamed of themselves, and wholly ashamed of the thing— amazed, but still endeavouring to console themselves with the old drone of their duty — moving about uneasily, almost afraid to show their heads or to be seen of men, peering out anxiously on the altered state of things. Alas, poor battered monkery! around them the smoke of the late cannonade, social eclipse, and stumbling at every step—no prospect— irremediable blight, alienation, and heart-eating gloom! Beyond their unhappy walls, Cromwell and his Ironsides, and the whole host, with banner and trumpet, filling the blue vault of heaven with the sound of their jubilant retreat!

It was a time of excitement, a time of much figure of speech; the symbolical vocabulary was enlarged, and many new expressions were added. What occasional hearer does not still remember his astonishment at much of the language of the new pulpits in and for some time after that memorable 1843, or heard without saying to himself,

"This is very extraordinary! this profusion of metaphor, this unlimited fervency of language—this exalted reprobation of the old leaven, the horrid old Residuary period past! I cannot doubt its sincerity, but is it quite rational?—nay, is it in the right direction? Does it point to some higher and better state of meaning beyond these disturbed times—

> To that deep azure of the settled mind,
> Calm looking down and permanent?

or will it continue thus labouring up for years, clouds of words driving before the wind, with only glimpses of rest between, casting a distant glory, so to speak, over the desired haven of peace on earth and good will to men ?"

Such were the sort of questions asked by many persons among the on-looking dissenting bodies, men of sound sense and undoubted piety, who wished well to the movement. For there really was something grand about it. It seemed like a rekindling of the national ashes—a revival of the old beau ideal belief in a perfect National Church, for which Scotland had so long struggled.

It is not our business here to inquire how far the movement has kept its promise. That there have been short-comings is admitted, though no candid person will believe the number so great as stated in

Doctor Dom. Jejustso of New Cuthberts his book, because such tables must obviously, in the nature of things, be of doubtful composition. Look in, for example, any day you are passing, on the reverend and new-made doctor, by this time somedele corpulent and waxing in the wane—see him gratefully fatigued, returning from his parochial rounds to the novelty of a plentiful table, the actual realisation of many a youthful, long-forgotten dream; how natural for the doctor, after dinner, to sit down and write *such good accounts of the Church*, founded on little hearsay stories picked up among his people in the course of the day's calls. Here a deserter returned to the fold; there a whole family! Every man, unless he were wholly given over to apathy and indolence, felt bound to defend his own body according to what was in him.

But, leaving the doctor to his statistics, a more affecting consideration, I submit, to the reader, may be traced in the deep disappointment that overtook some, and not the least earnest, who, at the outset, were as the sons and daughters of the morning. The Hallow Isle Tragedy, the story of which we are now to relate, occurred in a remote locality, and had but a slender and imperfect connexion with the great movement just spoken of; it might have happened equally under any other form of secession—nay, in the bosom of the Church itself—had it been "laid upon" the lady who plays the principal part in the story to rout her family on the old ground.

It was, then, on a chilly evening in May, during the Assembly week of 1843, that a young man, with a parcel under his arm, might have been seen has-

tening eastward along Princes-street; his
watch, it appeared by the West Kirk clock,
had deceived him five minutes, and he was
afraid of losing the last coach to Lasswade,
in which direction his journey lay.

The traveller's black dress and white
neckcloth bespoke him a clergyman; his
youth, haste, unusually grave face, and
awkwardness at his parcel, so different
from the experienced Presbyter's manner
of dandling *his* city purchases as he strode
along the same street, all betrayed the
embryo pastor in his probationary stage of
dominiehood.   He had the air of poverty,
too, so long inseparable from the black
coat: his figure, which was of the middle
height, it is impossible to say much about
at present without reference to a better
tailor: as rendered by the village artist,
whose board was next door to the school-
house where the young man laboured, it

struck you as being a little too short in the legs, or, as the bucks would say, queer.

Still there was an interesting look about the young man—an interest difficult to define. His face would have been handsome, but that in the thoughtful earnestness of the expression there seemed to lurk a tinge of discontent; and the chin a little too long, though nothing to Dr. Oates's, seemed to intimate the same undue fear and hatred of popery, or rather the tendency that way; for as yet the feature, thanks to the natural modesty and grace of youth, had not acquired that degree of prominence.

To conclude our brief sketch, poor Logan Morland thought himself good-looking.

He arrived at the coach-stand; the coach was gone. It is needless to say how bitter were his feelings. The unfortunate little chronometer (an heirloom descended from his great-grandfather) was produced and convicted by the Register clocks; his look of unutterable agony will suggest itself at once to every good-natured reader, when he thus found himself, after wandering the streets of Edinburgh all day, reduced to a still further walk of some ten or eleven miles ere he could reach his present home in the Chapel hills beyond Roslyn.

But there was no choice to one whose poverty barely enabled him to maintain the coat on his back; he could not afford to pay for a night's board and lodging in town; besides, to say the truth, he was in no mood to tolerate the capital by night with its Babylonish glare and noise, its filled taverns and theatres, its streets traversed by smoking puppies, three, four, and five abreast, and swarming with harlots. So, having recruited the wearied energies of nature with a slight refreshment at a moderate eating-house near the college, Logan Morland set out on his long walk home.

And that too in the blindness and agony of one who had just had the cherished hope of his life extinguished—his very eyes, so to speak, put out. It would be no easy matter to give a correct picture of his reflections. A stunning sense of fatigue and horrible disappointment combined, prompted him ever and anon to mend his pace (people stared to see a person of his cloth walking apparently for a wager), and in the more solitary turns of the road, when he could do so unobserved, to break out into a short run. Mingled, too, with the subject at present on his mind, and towering at times over all, rose the contrast of the late paternal home. In the sublime figure of Ossian, the young man might have said, "My father's ghost appeared to me on the hill; the stars dim twinkled through his form."

The memory of his late parent, the stern old Cameronian merchant of the Salt-market, seemed to follow him in the darkening twilight, while the chill wind gave, as it were, voice and utterance to the remonstrating Shade. "Son, why this unseemly haste? is this thy Christian fortitude ere I am twelve months cold in the grave?" And the tears started to the young man's eyes; but no tear fell, for he was not of that kind. Poor fellow, no wonder he was deeply moved. That morning he had walked into town to claim his recommendation to the vacant parish of ——, of which he had the promise from his spiritual chief; he had seen his chief, and his chief had told him he was not to have it; his chief had told him he was to COME OUT. An appalling sentence to poor Logan Morland.

Although possessed of fair average abilities, our young preacher's was not a mind to grapple with such a crisis as was then pending. He had paid but little attention to the controversy in its preliminary stages; he had thought it but a passing flaw. What else could it appear to him, toiling away out there at his preparatory school drudgery? And now it burst upon him wholly unprepared. He was somehow *not in the secret* on either side; it came like the intimation of the Deluge of old: Behold the fountains of the deep were breaking up, and he was left out of the ark. It never, for example, occurred to him to beguile the pain and weariness of his walk home with the reflection that by-and-by there would be kirks going, snug vacancies over which his chief had no control. Had such a reflection occurred distinctly to him, it would probably have altered in an instant the whole colour of the young man's career; had his foresight, I say, been able to perceive the lights which time has since rekindled over that dark and troubled body, Logan was just the man to have sat down among the Residuaries. When it did occur to him, as will be seen further on, he was too deeply compromised to follow his own inclination in disobedience to the stern rebuke of his chief: "What, sir! would you take your place among a disgraced and inferior priesthood, made up of the refuse of a corrupt Church, and the leavings of our parish schools?" Able men these chiefs. With arguments like that, addressed to the piety of the old and the vanity of the young, no wonder they drew so many after them.

It was past ten o'clock, and all but quite dark, when our wearied pedestrian sighted his home in that small chain of hills lying to the south of Roslyn. Indescribable was the pang at once of pleasure and of pain when his eye first caught the light in the window of their cottage. A cold east wind whistled through the few and still half-naked patches of plantation, ringing yet sharper against the hills as the school-master neared his abode, a solitary cottage standing pretty high up the ridge. A single light, as I have just said, shone in its small casement. Logan sighed, lifted the latch, and entered.

His sister rose to meet him. " Oh, Logan, what has kept you so late ?" She looked anxiously in his face : " It is, then, as I feared—you are not to get it ?"

" Yes," returned he, peevishly, " it is as you were always ready enough to prophesy

—I am not to have it—actually not to have it. Some prophecies, they say, have a tendency to fulfil themselves."

A few ill-concealed tears were the only refutation of the absurd and groundless charge ;. but, after all, the disappointment was a heavy one, and there was some excuse for his being a little absurd and unreasonable.

"Did you see Doctor Standish?" inquired his sister, drying her eyes.

"Yes, I saw them both—both Standish and Konigdom."

A momentary but scared smile appeared in the sister's eyes at his peevish way of mentioning these mighty names : Standish, a pillar and a flaming sword ; Konigdom, a kingdom of a man, burly and massive, the nucleus of a host.

He was silent, and did not seem in-

clined to enter into further particulars that
night.

"Shall I get you something to eat,
Logan? You must," said the sister, "be
both tired and hungry."

"I should think so!" said our friend,
taking off his shoes. "I was too late for
the coach, and had to walk the whole way.
Where are my slippers?"

"Walk the whole way!" echoed Effie.
"Cruel! and you so unused to walk—
after you had walked *in* to have to walk
out again! Shall I make you a little
warm negus?"

"Gruel you must mean," replied Logan;
"they make negus with wine."

Poor Effie burst into tears at this awk-
ward and ill-timed blunder. Wine was of
course a luxury unknown to the house-
keeping of the poor teacher, and this was

the first time since their father's death that
she had tripped, and forgot for the moment
they had no longer the comforts of the
old home. The bitter fountain, once set
a flowing, would not be stayed.

" Effie," said the young preacher, in a
tone of more affectionate solemnity, " how
often must I have to check you for these
sinful and unavailing outbursts ? Do you
think, you foolish girl, that I really care
about wine ? A morsel of bread and milk,
or any trifle you have in the house, will
suffice. I am too tired to give you the particulars of this most unfortunate journey
of mine to-night, but you shall hear all to-
morrow."

His sister observed that to-morrow was
Sunday ; our wearied friend said he was
aware of that, and, desiring her to go to
bed, he was left alone to his frugal supper.

CHAPTER II.

THE MORNING WALK TO CHURCH.

EFFIE, who was rather a pretty brunette, differed as widely from her brother in temper and disposition as in outward appearance ; he was at once talkative or reserved, according to his company, variable and inclined to despondency, but somewhat sturdy withal ; she was of a more even and cheerful temper, with something of a cast of humour inclining to take to her humble lot if better might not be. In their common struggle against poverty she

c 2

failed altogether to come up to Logan's standard. Not all his seven college years' apprenticeship to the acquirement of a pure English pronunciation could cure Effie of her native Doric; day after day, though knowing better, she persisted in saying shrewd things in the mother tongue, so that our parson, who did indeed admit that his sister possessed the rudiments of a lady, was daily provoked with her agaceries. Devout, or, at all events, strictly correct in his sentiments, he was so close, it was difficult to say what precisely Logan's piety was; while poor Effie had to undergo many a fraternal lecture on her neglect of form, and her indifference to the higher mysteries, and her natural goodness of heart, which our friend said was carnal. While Logan, in short, took after the old Salt-market merchant their father, a rigid true blue Covenanter,

Effie was wholly her poor mother's, who had so little sense of her danger as a sinner, that nothing (the senior Morland was wont to affirm to his children) short of the last trumpet would awaken her to it. Effie probably thought this a hard sentence of the old gentleman's. " Who could bear it ?" And from a very early age she had sagacity enough to perceive that, to all practical intents and purposes, her mother was as good a woman as the old gentle⸱ man was a man. But this opinion she modified in after years : their father, with his amount of austere self-denial, was a character that no child could comprehend.

Thus was the difference of the parents reproduced in the children, but softened by transmission and the influence of that stroke which sent them abroad on the world mutually dependent upon each other for bread and a home. The frivolity which,

in the somewhat worldly Glasgow dame,
was so distasteful to the good man of the
Salt-market, was in the penniless sister of
the poor preacher pretty well kept under
the rod; and there was this further difference, that, whereas the ancient Saunders
was to some extent set at nought by his
light better-half, Effie was wholly devoted
to her brother, and the more so, that he
had his faults. This, by the way, was
rather a sore point with our parson (I call
him so now, because he was found in everything fitting to sustain the character, save
a kirk): he had a secret nibbling suspicion that his sister, in her estimate of
him, dared to stop short of perfection.
She certainly did so. His dogmatism and
turn for polemics might be highly ac-
counted of as a virtue entitling him to a
place in the host then assembled at Edinburgh, but at home Effie called it by its

right name, without, however, abating a
jot of her sisterly regard. And Logan, on
his part, had inherited, along with the
sterner attributes of his father, a slight
tincture of the maternal vacillation which,
if it did not make him more tolerant in
his opinions, certainly rendered him much
less of a despot in practice than the old
Salt-market merchant, who had stalked
through life as if he still smelt the gun-
powder of Bothwell Brig. So also in the
matter of personal appearance; while
Logan retained to some slight extent the
peaked and uplifted chin of his sire, he inherited, in common with Effie, the milder
eyes of their poor mother. There was but
one exception to the parallel in the matter
of stature, Effie's slender, graceful figure
having attained to the perfect height of
girlhood, tall, but not too tall, whereas
our parson inclined to the short and

sturdy. With this preliminary sketch of our hero and heroine, we leave the minuter shades of character to be gathered from the narrative.

Sunday morning came, and, behold! the wind was no longer singing with chill and sterile croon at Effie's small casement which looked into the east; it was away round to the west—a lovely May morning, with just one flock of white clouds in the heavens' "delicious blue"—such a morning as made my old friend, Dr. Malagrub, who was something crazed with study, poor man, exclaim "he could run stark naked in for joy."

Brother and sister set out on their accustomed walk to church. But the sound of the church-going bell, and the putting forth of bud and herbage, and the quiet dewy hills, and the tearful beauty of everything, more clearly brought out by the day of rest, were in great measure thrown away on our parson, whose natural taste for such things was at no time exuberant, and at present his mind was engrossed with other thoughts. They walked for some time in silence, the distance to church being considerable. Effie made no allusion to his yesterday's journey, not from any lack of curiosity to hear the particulars, but she was averse to introduce a discussion of so painful a nature, having every reason to believe that her brother was far from being in a frame to speak temperately of his disappointment. On a text of that kind he was apt to speak louder than quite befitted the morning walk to church, with echo on the outlook to catch up every sound, and the fields and footpaths, to use the poet's expression, sprinkled with church-going company. At length Logan introduced it himself—not beginning at the beginning, but at the point he had previously reached in his reflections.

"The more I think of it," he said, "the more I am at a loss to find any excuse for this unaccountable treatment of me by Standish and Konigdom. After buoying me up with the hope of ——, to turn round all at once and say I am not to have it!"

"The impending change in the Church, perhaps," suggested Effie.

Effie was careful to avoid the agaceries on Sunday, and spoke nearly as pure a style as the parson himself.

"Whose fault is that?—not mine," he continued. "What, I say, has my personal and individual usefulness to do with this outbreak? If, a year ago, Standish thought me an eligible successor to the second charge at ——, where's the mighty difference now? There's none ethically, that I can see."

"Nor I," said Effie. "It *is* hard to give up all thought of a pretty, retired place, like ——, that we have so long looked forward to." (Logan smiled at Effie's notion of the ethics of the case.) "Oh, brother, you will never think of going abroad! Promise me that you will not turn a missionary. I read such a miserable account the other day in a letter to Mary Fletcher from her brother."

"What should put that in your head?" said Logan, a little sharply. "That certainly will be the last thing I'll think of. I hope, my good sister, it has not quite come to that with me yet; it must be a small bushel at home I would not prefer to that. But, in the mean time, my good Effie, can you tell me what I am to do to get myself and you bread? I'll teach

no longer, that I am determined; neither,
it appears to me, will my staying at home
mend their breach of faith; it won't give
me ———."

"Indeed that is true," Effie admitted.
"But surely, Logan—think of our father!
There must be some independent course,
let people say what they will. Either you
belong to this change, or you do not; and
surely there must be some good reason for
so many good men going out with such
preachers as Dr. Standish and Dr. Konigdom, and many others at their head."

"I don't know that," said our friend,
moodily; "small thing often stirs the multitude, and the poor are too often the
readiest to follow; I say, sister, it is their
very numbers that makes me suspicious of
them. And must come out too! not, will
you come? I must say it sounds odd to

tell a man he must come out who has never been in."

The epigrammatic quibble imposed upon Effie, and she admitted it was odd.

"They might, at least," continued Logan, "have given me some premonition or warning beforehand of all this, if they expected to carry me along with them. Did they suppose that while I was attending to their school drudgery out here I was keeping pace with themselves?"

"Perhaps they might," said Effie. "So much now-a-days is left to the newspapers——"

"The newspapers!" cried the parson, indignantly; "those pernicious incendiaries, who never can see a smoke anywhere but they must take the bellows to blow it into a flame."

"For mercy's sake, speak lower, Logan."

" What," moderating his tone, " were
the newspapers, without a sufficient motive
to interest me in the question? and besides, I don't care for newspaper reading.
All very well for those who have anything
to lose to read the newspapers—I don't
wonder at *their* feeling anxious."

" No, indeed, poor creatures ! I hear,"
said Effie, " that a great many of them are
preparing to leave their kirks. That cannot be for nothing, Logan. If you are so
set upon a place you never had, what must
be their feelings to leave a place where
they have grown old ?"

" It was doubtless a very great hard-
ship," our friend said, " but he did not see
what that had to do with the question. If
they felt the command to go out to be so
imperative, they were right to go, but in
what respect was their going out binding
upon him ?"

"Surely in no respect, unless it were the natural desire to share in the affliction, and go where so many good men were going," Effie said.

"Effie," said the brother, seriously, "you speak at times like a mere senseless fool. I do not apply the taunt to *you*, but I know that there are many to whom that same sharing in other people's affliction is their greatest luxury: the question is its utility. What could my sharing in their affliction do? The Master will judge by the masters' work, and it is no infallible proof that it is work because it is set about weeping. Understand. I trust I know how to make a sacrifice as well as another; but I say that the unknown destination of an uncertain movement holds out to my individual usefulness a poor exchange for a known and ascertained sphere. That is the gist I complain of. Had they

taken things more coolly. But now they
have brought the Church to such a pass
that it has become a very nice question,
and there are many, I believe, who, like
myself, feel that they can neither, so to
speak, go out nor remain in."

"Is there any real disgrace in remaining
in?" asked Effie.

"Why, as to that, Effie," said the parson
—Logan sometimes condescended to droll
a little—"not having a kirk myself I cannot exactly say. I believe there is a sort
of general impression to that effect; but
I think I know one, that if he were in,
would make it go hard with them to prove
the disgrace of remaining."

"But you *are* in," said the simple Effie,
"unless, indeed, you passed your word to
them yesterday in Edinburgh?"

"Catch me! They would fain have
brought me to that, but I gave them to

understand they had no such simpleton to deal with. Bland, indeed, was little short of disgusting."*

" Then why distress yourself, brother— why go out ? If you do not feel it to be your duty, you are not bound to do what Mr. Bland bids you, or Dr. Standish either."

" My simple sister, how little you know of the matter ! Have you forgotten that my sole patronage is derived through Standish ? You don't suppose, do you, that the doctor will appoint me to the choice of their vacant pulpits the moment they flee to the hills ?"

---

* There was but too much of this. A worthy, though rather weak man, minister of the second charge in an inland parish, being "*persuaded*" to take the pledge, his wife sent the beadle next day, with their nine children, to say that Mr. ——, on his return home, " *had been better advised.*" So the story went. The conjugal sentence was commuted next morning to the minister's being instructed to write to that effect—threatening them with the beadle, &c.

"No!" replied Effie, with some spirit; "but neither, I suppose, will the doctor fly off with the patronage of all the vacant pulpits in his pocket."

"Ha!" said Logan, "you touch the matter there—there's something in that, Effie. And yet," relapsing into the boding tone, "I don't know—there will be such a rabble of applicants."

Their proximity to the church cut short a discussion which certainly did not promise to be of much profit; and Logan took his seat with the tacit resolution of being guided, in some measure, by the views of Mr. ——, who, it was generally understood, would that day feel called upon to declare himself to his congregation.

But Mr. —— did not preach; he was still detained in Edinburgh at head-quarters, and a stranger mounted the pulpit. He was a young man full of zeal in the cause, sent out for the purpose of sounding the congregation—one of those ardent youths of the period, whose fluent, unhesitating oratory told upon the country flocks.

Now Logan Morland was not fluent : he was a hesitating speaker ; and had it depended on the weight he attached to that lad's exhortations, he most assuredly would not have come out. On their way home he criticised the sermon sharply to Effie, and did not scruple to call his youthful contemporary (Effie rather admired him) a ranting, democratic puppy, and spoiled sub-editor of a provincial journal, full of sound and fury, signifying nothing. "But when the deep floods are up," added he, "we must expect the froth to fly in our

face now and then"—thereby giving the
first dim intimation of his intention of
going out, or rather, perhaps, of his
foreboding that he would be obliged
to go.

CHAPTER III.

LOGAN IS SUMMONED TO THE CONVENTION—MEETS AN OLD
ACQUAINTANCE IN PRINCES-STREET, WHO ENDEAVOURS TO
DISSUADE HIM FROM GOING NEAR—HIS APPOINTMENT TO
THE PASTORSHIP OF HALLOW.

BUT time was pressing on the great
event, and that in turn drawing upon all
its resources. A summons from his chief
put an end to my friend's unprofitable in-
decision, and mounting an early evening
coach at the nearest stage of Lasswade,
Logan was again set down in the busy
city.

It was the night before the march to

Cannon Mills. As he hurried along Princes-street, gay and crowded as usual with the varied population of the metropolis, all at once, at the corner of —— street, an odd-looking, peremptory Doubt or Shape of shabby appearance, stopped him with the suddenness of a footpad leaping out of a ditch. " This movement," it said, " is it the great thing they fancy? or a distinction without a difference? I perceive, sir, you don't at this moment recollect me. I am Professor ——! Permit me, my young friend, to take you by the elbow. What," asks the Shadow, pointing its plausible horns *with* the great life stream (chiefly westward in the evening)—" what is this elect composition in the pound you are going to—what to that gaily-dressed crowd of people who, I will lay you a wager, are at this moment all joking and laughing at it?"

But here my friend, clearly perceiving the cloven foot, had the sense and resolution at once to break off so dangerous a conference; as poor almost as himself, he saw what the devil would be at. Still, like most inexperienced young men of stoical temper and orthodox opinions, who look chiefly to the surface of society, Morland's views of the religious element were very limited, and so mixed up with school drudgery, it was scarcely possible for him to think of the one without the other. Of its specific gravity and moral qualities as an element I suspect my friend knew very little, if, indeed, anything at all—nothing of its depth and buoyancy, nothing of the countless human hearts (sin bubbles) wandering in it for ever and ever. He could count the complacent few sitting in their creeds on the surface, and that was all.

At the meeting of Council, to which he

had been invited, he heard the speeches of
the leaders; and cold and dubious though
he was, he could not altogether resist the
fervour and animation of these extraordinary men. He began to feel his own
superficiality. When the meeting broke
up, and his chief, at parting, pressed his
hand and said, " *Well?*"—significant mo-
nosyllable!—Logan, more frankly than
belonged to his character, replied, "Ah,
doctor! with a little of your eloquence I
would not care where I went. I—I'll take
another night to think of it."

But here let me record a conversation
which led more immediately to the adop-
tion of our hero. The scene is a smaller
meeting, assembled in a handsome draw-
ing-room in the new town, in the house
of a wealthy and distinguished citizen of
Edinburgh. The company are chiefly
clergymen. In the group to which the

reader's attention is invited a certain persuasive clergyman of the city (Mr. Bland)
has been employed to talk over an influential but wavering Boanerges (Mr. Rand)
from the far north.

Pursuing his inquiries how they were all
in Sutherland—"And when," says Mr.
Bland, " did you see our Hallow Isle
friends? Do they intend sending the
younger lads south to college, do you
know?"

Mr. Rand, with just a tinge of north
country accent, said, in reply: " I know
nothing of the lads' movements. But I
hear the old man, the laird, is in a very
poorly way, and not like to live long."

" So I was exceedingly sorry to hear,"
returned he of Edinburgh. " Good old
man! the last conversation I had with
him when he was south he was decidedly
with us—I fear we may not hope as much

from his son, the young laird : *his* college
education, by the way, did him no good.
Melethor Deerness, I am told, has turned
out as proud and conceited as might have
been prognosticated from his barbarous
and absurd Christian name. If he sides
with any at all, it will be with the Voluntaries of Kirkwal and the mainland; or,
what is just as likely, he may make a
stand on the Residuary side, and join his
stiff-necked cousin, Caldwel Gilchrist."

"Hold you there," whispers Rand;
"there may go two words to that bargain.
The mother, I am informed, has declared
on our side (in the event, that is, of my
taking on with you), and she is one in
earnest, I can tell you. Between ourselves,
the Lady of Hallow is a powerful wöman;
she is like the rock in the desert that was
smitten by the wand of the prophet—stop

the gush who can ! I doubt if we should have touched her."

"Explain yourself, my dear sir," says the other, inclining his head gently.

"I told you," said Mr. Rand, "the old laird's removal is looked for daily at the ingle-cheek. They say he has that upon his mind which it is ill to keep and harder still to part with; and who can tell how the old man's decease may affect her? I say it is just possible, when you think to get in your hand, and graft your consolation upon *that*, a sudden change of mind or delutch of grief might sweep the whole deputation God kens whar !"

"Hush!" says Mr. B., a little alarmed at this robust language. "I know—I am aware—that our friend is a woman of warm and impulsive feelings. But you used an expression a little ago which sur-

prised me. My dear sir, what do you
mean by *something on the old man's
mind?"*

Rand, it should be stated here, had
through Mrs. Rand a small estate in Orkney, and was therefore an Orkney laird;
he made no claim, indeed, to rank with the
larger proprietors, and being a clergyman
of the Church of Scotland in an overlooking aristocratic county, there was no need
that he should do so; but he still, long
after the romance had worn off his acquirement of Finnigand, continued to feel and
to cherish a warm side towards his insular
neighbours across the Frith. Socially,
therefore, he was much better acquainted
with the Orkney families, including this of
Hallow, than Bland was, that gentleman's
connexion being, as the northern divine
conceived, of rather a flimsy description.

In reply to his question concerning the

dying old laird, the reverend member for Sutherland answered with reluctance, his hard-favoured visage exhibiting in its central feature the true Celtic horn :

" Egh! uigh! umph!" he grunted, " I should not have mentioned that ; because, upon the whole, the facts are not very well known, and out of respect to the family the subject is seldom or never spoken of— never at least among the educat' class; if it is kept alive at all it's over the peat fires of the small tenantry and the yattering natives of the isles themselves. It's just an old gousty tradition."

" Of which, however," said Mr. Bland, " you can give me an outline. I take a deep interest in the family."

The young laird boarded with Bland when at college, and the younger lads were expected ; that was about the extent and depth of his interest, so far as Mr. Rand was aware. Mr. Rand: "Since you are importunate, sir; but recollect, it can only be an outline.

"There are two versions, then, my goot sir, which pretend to give an account of why and wherefore it is that this dying old laird sits hanging his head in the chimley-cheek rather than take to his bed. The first is, that his wife, this same Mrs. Deerness, that's called Lady of Hallow, occupees the shoes of another woman!"

"What!" cries Mr. Bland, "bigamy! Do you mean that Mr. Deerness, of Hallow——"

"No, no, no, no!" cries Highland Rand, in his turn; "you fly away so fast, my tear sir! I did not say that, nor did ever the tradition : the meaning is that he was engaged, and under the bonds of natur', to another woman when he married this one."

Bland's fine countenance fell a little at this piece of information, but he made no comment.

"The other version," proceeded Mr. Rand, "is hardly worth mentioning, it goes so far back into the mists of by-past generations, when the family was first founded in these isles; although, as an antiquarian, I know more of this *fama dolorosa* than I do of the other. But it must be all nonsense—an idle, fanciful legend, made up after the old monkish pattern, that would pretend to divide this same Hallow estate and give half to the kirk! In times so modern as these I doubt, Mr. Bland, that day of miracle's past!"

"Do not think so, my dear sir," says the enthusiastic Bland. "Say rather that that day is returning with signs and with——"

Rand, dryly: "If you think so—and

can take an old battered legent as confirmation current of your prospects in the
north, I shall not, my dear sir, withhold
from you the sconce to scour. This that
we are now speaking of is considerably
more than a hundred years old. You
must know that these Deernesses of Hallow
were not at one time the sole lords of the
manor. Though come of the same stock,
originally there were two proprietors in
the island, until one by maistery, or by
cunning and lending of siller—at all events
in some way or other—got the upper hand
of his weaker neighbour, and made a
sheeled peascod of him, which, as the story
goes, procured for the denuded laird the
euphonious cognomen of Lugs. Well, sir,
this Lugs was not so deficient of insight as
they thought, for he prophesied before he
died that a day would come when this
family suld be smitten for the iniquity of

their forebear, and the ill-gotten gear gang the old road—videlicet, scattered to the winds, or else be given to the kirk !"

" I see you laugh at this as an idle legend," said Mr. Bland; "but what if I happen to know something of this Lugs' prophecy, and can show you its probable interpretation !"

Rand: " Oh ! you refer, I suppose, to the pop'lar belief that the weird is to be fulfilled in this present man's time. I am aware there is a prevalent opinion that old Hallow (who, between ourselves, is much such another as Lugs of the tradition) intends, contrar both to the wish of his wife and of his man of business, to split the property and to set up, in the abstracted moiety thus restored, his second son and namesake the lad Weatherby, notwithstanding that the young man is little better than a gomeril. But this, I suspect, is all imagination—all the fond conceit and superstition of a small ignorant tenantry sitting yattering to one another by the ingle-lowe over their departing laird's state of his worldly affairs and settlements."

" Is this young man Weatherby so deficient ?"

" There is plenty of him," said Rand; "the lad is of goodly stature, but he is not such as I would look out for a daughter of mine, supposing my lambies were come that length."

Mr. Bland coughed and coloured; did the Highland catamountain know that Miss Bland was eighteen ?

They were here joined by other reverend acquaintances, and the conversation on the subject of Hallow Isle became more general. One wished to know whether it was true that the incoming laird—the

Master of Hallow, as they conceitedly affected to call him in Kirkwal—had taken to free thinking? bluntly answered by Rand in the negative "No!" Another feared there was no chance of carrying their minister, old Calthrop, of Corbysholm cum Hallow. The *Doctor* was at him this morning, but "he seems utterly insensible and determined to stick to his island." Mr. Rand did not much wonder at that. "Crawtaes has been too long there to change. The truth is, they are but a kind of half salvages yet, these men of the isles. You haf no conception of their ignorance; you would think, to hear them yatter, that the very winds of heafen, which, to say the truth, beat for ever on their coasts, had blown the poor creatures doited. But it is getting late, and I must go before the shops shut, as I haf some purchases to make."

E 2

And the Doctor looking in upon them in the course of the evening, Mr. Bland took the opportunity of laying the case before the chief.

" Certainly, Mr. Bland," was the reply, "everybody and every place is of import- ance just now ; if possible, not the remotest pendicle should be overlooked. I think, however, you should avoid discussing re- mote points with Rand, he is not the man; in his present undecided mood they are too dangerously suggestive." And here the Doctor, after the fatigues of the day, indulged a little. " You have heard that absurd story he tells of his cousin Peter, who ran away the night before Waterloo, solely and accidentally, as Peter on his un- looked for appearance at home stated, from his happening to hear a drummer- boy singing at a little distance the " Blue- bells of Scotland." We must have a care

Rand does not imitate his cousin's *amor patriæ*. In your ear, my dear Bland, this is the greatest fear I have. Our Sutherland friend is not the only Rand in our ranks. I much fear when it comes to it we have a few who will hear the drummerboy sing by night, who will not wait to hear him beat the drum in the morning. How often, alas, does the courage in small bulk put to shame our larger men! Peter Longlegs is on his way home to his mother, and the little drummer-boy lies dead on Waterloo. But in this of Hallow Isle the chief difficulty is where to get a man to send."

" There are still," suggested Bland, " a number of our young men on the unappointed list."

" Oh, I am aware of that," said the Doctor, " but the young man that we send to Hallow must have something in him—

some wear, some endurance. Ah! I have
it! there's my young friend Logan Morland, out at Chapel-end, is just the very
man."

And so Logan's destiny was settled. In
vain he started objections, raised stipula-
tions; his impatient chief heard him to an
end, a feat for which, to say the truth, the
great Doctor was not at all times remarkable; but, like a skilful angler with his
trout, he was determined to land Morland,
and he landed him. He was to sail for
Orkney in September. And Mr. Bland, in
the mean time, was empowered and requested to see to the necessary negotia-
tions with the Lady of Hallow.

Logan Morland became at once an ac-
tive, zealous, and even keen free churchman. Small wits may find matter to scoff
at in this, but they are quite mistaken. A
young preacher, with hitherto no fixed

creed in church politics, might have been excused for taking any side; it was to Logan's credit that he took what in his heart he thought the right side, the side his rigid old father would have taken, had he been alive.

There was much in the destined scene of his labours calculated to impress the fancy of Morland; with his constitutional tendency to the sombre side of things, the remoteness of these islands and their semi-barbarous condition went a long way: they implied power to the civiliser, and Logan loved power. His interim meditations, therefore, partook unusually of the delectable, and much pre-uplifted was he with the great things to be done among the benighted descendants of ancient Thule.

It was natural, too, that he should wish to learn something respecting the family who formed the chief society of the island. And on this point his curiosity received rather an unexpected fillip.

One Saturday, being in town, he was in Daidle the bookseller's shop. Daidle's was the pet lounge, a sort of *popina sacerdotalis*, where you were always sure to meet with some of them if you wished to hear the news, or to take a sniff at the last new books. But much depended on the hour. It was the stilly, or clerical dinner hour, when our friend called to make his purchases, and there was nobody in the shop but the venerable bibliopolist himself. His parcel of stationery made up, Logan naturally spoke of his appointment to Hallow, when Mr. Daidle, his venerable white head gently oscillating, looked him fixedly in the face for several moments, and then said to him, with an air of much sweetness and solemnity,

" Perhaps I could tell you something of the family at Hallow that would surprise you, Mr. Morland."

Logan of course said, " Indeed ?"

" Yes," continued Mr. Daidle. Mr. Daidle's voice was singularly sonorous and well adapted to such legends; it had a sort of far-off, plaintive sound, that reminded you of the cooing of wood-pigeons in a wood. " There was once," said Mr. Daidle, " in the large provincial town I come from, a wealthy merchant, Harry Gordon Baron. He was a man, as far as money and money's command went, perfect before the world, just and punctual in his dealings, but an utter ultra, you must understand, sir, in all other respects; high and haughty of temper, no society was good enough for him. This Harry Gordon Baron had a numerous family of daughters, who, as the saying went, failed their papa nothing, for no man was good enough for them; and even so befel them, Mr. Morland—Harry Gordon Baron died bankrupt, and the poor things were scattered to the world. Alicia, or Sally, the youngest——"

In short, Mr. Daidle told him the whole story of poor Sally Baron, which will be found further on in its proper place; how she went as a governess to Orkney in the family of Mr. Gilbert Greenlaw, of Green-law, and should have been married to Mr. Deerness, but his friends put him past her with a falsely concocted report of insanity in the Gordon Baron family; and how the cruel usage and disappointment did drive the poor thing a little light-headed, so that she was still to this day a fugitive and a wanderer in a weary world. Moreover, how it was said that the good-natured laird, when he found out the trick they had played him, swore an oath by his

Maker that he would give "some of their hearts a thraw for that yet."

" I have not," said Mr. Daidle, in conclusion, " the honour to know much of the lady that fills my poor townswoman's place: I may say I have seen her, and that's all; but"—Mr. Daidle here paused with a peculiarly solemn oscillation of the head, and then said—" I thought I would tell you."

" And the corollary you would have me draw from this narrative, Mr. Daidle?" inquired Logan.

But Mr. Daidle did not deal in corollaries; with something of a foolish look, if one may say so of so venerable-looking a man, he merely repeated what he had already said: "I thought it might be interesting to you to know something of the family."

Logan had not quite so very high an opinion of Mr. Daidle as some of his more advanced brethren had; but, upon the whole, he concluded the narrative was intended as a friendly hint to him not to expect the path in his present contemplated outgoings to be entirely strewed with roses. He was content to accept the hint. So far as that went, Logan Morland, at four-and-twenty, had done with the roses; what he now desired and wanted was a change of the thorns.

His mind made up to go, he was surprised to find how little he had to lose by the change. At Chapel-end he had scarcely an acquaintance; no attachments, no prospects, no friends to part with; nothing but that noisy hovel where he kept school, next door to Wauch the tailor, a descendant of the celebrated Mansie of Dalkeith, a pestilent fellow, and more given to argument than his grandfather. Just fancy

the tailor before eleven o'clock in the fore-
noon, half naked from his shopboard,
sauntering into the school-house, openly
defying the unhappy teacher to impugn
some new thesis or theory, the production
of his persevering noddle, and from premise to conclusion as absurd and unfitting
as the garments he made! No wonder
Logan was glad of any change which promised to remove him from the visitations
of so horrible a spectre.

But it was otherwise with Effie, who
had formed attachments of one kind and
another not a few. It was the last day of
August when Logan, having at length
fully made up his mind, told her that they
were to go. Effie heard, and fled with the
disastrous intelligence to her dear friend
Mary Fletcher.

"Oh, Mary, woman, what have I to tell

you! My brother's ordered to Orkney: we are to sail in September, and the morn's the first."

"To Orkney!" cried Effie's friend, "that's far." And the two girls sat down and cried, and talked themselves round as best they could. Effie then proposed a walk.

"But put on your bonnet, Mary. I maun hae a walk wi' you—it may be the last we'll have—there's no security that Logan does not take it into his head to be off to-morrow."

"It's like a dream," said the farmer's buxom daughter, throwing on an old bon-grace of a bonnet that lay at hand—"like a dream," she repeated, and sauntered out with her friend without having once consulted the glass. And still, even when they were out of doors in the brilliant harvest weather, Mary Fletcher spoke like a person in a dream.

"Which way shall we go, up or down? But what does it signify? I see them shearing barley in the haugh."

"Up," said Effie. "I want to see Ben-Lomond and—and them all, and there's less chance of meeting anybody. I would not like it to be kenned just yet that we are going away."

"That's true," said Mary Fletcher. "It's no as if you were going to London on a jaunt."

"Oh, no, no!" said Effie.

Effie had one other dear friend to part with, an old bookseller who kept a small shop and circulating library in the next market village. Poor old Mr. John Davidson, or, as the children now called him,

Johnny—had once seen better days. He was originally a clergyman, seated in a living from which he was cruelly ejected on a frivolous charge of appearing tipsy in a friend's pulpit. The proof was second-hand, and totally insufficient. In those days it was enough to depose him, however, and John Davidson never drank a drop again. If it really was the case that he had lifted the cup which cost him so dear, like the dying king of ancient Thule, he cast it from him for ever. He turned bookseller in his native village. But now a rival and more showy establishment had drawn the public away from him, and Davidson sat in his deserted cell reading any dusty circulating volume that came to hand, circulating, alas ! no longer ; often the most important variation in his daily life being a child's purchase of a halfpenny picture-book. He had in these dark days one or two friends still on his shelves, and among them our Effie. He was much affected when Effie, entering the shop with the " Mysteries of Udolpho," told him she was going away. Tears filled the old man's eyes. " I'll miss you, my dear Miss Effie," said Mr. Davidson, " but I reckon it canna be helped, and changes, they say, are lightsome to young folk. I wish you weel, but you'll come and see me once more before you go. I would like to look out something, some little keepsake, and at present my head is sorely confused."

A few days afterwards, Effie called to see him again for the last time. He presented his keepsake, a small writing-desk, and took farewell of her in these simple, encouraging words : " It's no doubt a bare country that Orkney that you are

going to, Miss Effie, but there's a hantle
lairds about it, and who knows but we'll
next be hearing that you have picked up
one !"

CHAPTER IV.

THE VOYAGE.

" SORROW springeth up in the night, but joy cometh in the morning," is a truth as profound as it is beautiful. On that night of our travellers' removal into Edinburgh, after parting with so many friends, had any one told the parson's sister she would be quite well again in the morning, Effie would probably have rejected the consolation as being either a flattering or most satirical fib. And yet, to her surprise, she awoke early next morning in a strange

F 2

and silent hotel, and found it was the case.
Logan, who was up betimes and out for a
coach, returned rattling along the chilly
morning street with the needful vehicle.
Effie knew instinctively, by the clatter it
made, it could be none other; and in rather
less than an hour thereafter he found himself with his sister, his books, and the rest
of the parsonic baggage, on board the Kirkwal steamer lying at Granton Pier.

It was a fine, clear September morning;
the water, green and undulating in the
harbour outside, mirrored in the Frith
sail and sea-fowl, and, above all, each
cloud beheld its skyey image perfect. Six
or seven miles across lay the opposite coast,
with its scattered towns (the ancient cities
of Fife), historic remains, beautiful in the
distance, beautiful and most marvellously
distinct: and there were lots of passengers.
Everything smiled on the journey of the

young travellers, and combined to raise
their spirits. In the first place our envoy
had to see to his luggage, to its proper de-
positation and stowing away, a treat of itself
to the reverend mind. Then he had to run
up-stairs and down about a hundred little
matters; to acquaint himself with the
capabilities of the cabin; to admire the
handsome mirrors, and possibly, for a
passing moment, the reflexion therein; to
settle Effie's berth with the stewardess
with a brotherly solicitude that quite
charmed the matron of the main; to con-
sult the steward about his own, and to
inform him that he was the Reverend
Logan Morland, going to Hallow Isle—a
piece of information which truth compels
me to say seemed to make but little impression on the smoke-dried chamberlain
of the steamer; the man was either stupid
and did not understand, or else he was sunk

in utter indifference, but, as he had a woolly head, it was of the less consequence; so Logan bounced up to deck again to see that his luggage had not been tampered with in his absence, to take a critical inspection of his fellow-passengers, to ask Effie if she was not getting sick yet, and so on, until the widening gap between the crowded pier and the crowded deck and the boom of the engine-boilers apprised him that they were off.

Off! What a thrilling importance is often in that little fact. Now our friend was relieved of a certain sensation of insecurity that had beset him up to his last moment on *terra firma,* a sensation of its being just possible that even yet he might draw back, but now he was safe—a material link in the great chain that girds and binds up this world for eternity. Clerically, Logan saw few greater men on deck than

himself; and secularly, with all respect for
the ladies, barring puppies, and there were
a few on board, he was as pretty a piece
of flesh as any in Messina. Heaven forbid
we should ever cease to sympathise with
the boundless vanity of youth; it is honest
and in the right direction, on the way to
greater things. To have judged from our
friend's gait on deck that morning, an ob-
server might have thought him endowed
with the lion's heart and brain, or that he
fancied he was actually in person the great
chief himself.

Effie enjoyed the sail as only youngsters
enjoy such things—pure sensation undisturbed by a thought of self; or like some
older acquaintance of ours, the Reasoners
in a circle, quite content and happy to be
there, poor souls, she enjoyed the splendid
combination of sky and water and land
around her, and never asked where the

reverie was to end. Transcendently beautiful was the run along the Fife coast. It
was only when they were far enough out
to look back on the Chapel hills, or what
she took for them, that a temporary shade
came over Effie's handsome sunburnt face,
and she felt a swelling at the heart, occasioned by the thought of how lonely they
must now be to Mary Fletcher: would
she ever see Mary again?

How curiously different in different persons is the *modus operandi* of the affec-
tions. Our friend, too, looked back: when
I referred to the old tailor next door, and
said that Logan had formed no ties, I
rather overstated his peculiar idiosyncrasy;
friendship was certainly not his ruling
passion, still he had a few shares in that
romantic illusion (if I may call it so)
which gives life such a relish. There was
his brother pedagogue, Alfred Semple,

now the Reverend Alfred, just about to step into a neighbouring vacated living; often had the two young men taken sweet counsel together in the days of their domi-niehood; but now, when the sentimental whiff came over Logan, and he too looked back, behold! the Reverend Alfred had already ceased to miss him. Did not Logan see him dibbling leaks in his garden with the absorbed selfishness of a ten-year incumbent!

Our envoy then felt saddened at the short-coming of his friend. The only cure for this lay in a vigorous application to his present position and company. But, al-though he had the traveller's turn for ask-ing questions, and was wholly free from bashfulness, he was somehow deficient in the initiative grace, and it took him long to make the acquaintance of strangers; he was a little fastidious too—it was not every one he took to; moreover, it was not every one who would take to him; and in fine, like most young travellers, he had the exclusive whim (at present a little sharpened by the defection of the aforesaid Alfred) of running up an intimacy with some particular individual to the neglect of every other person on board, which would have been abominable were the favoured party some great man. But your green traveller is not at all nice in his choice; like your lover, he rather delighteth to let you see what he can do, and such a treasure our friend was at length so happy as to find. With this gentleman he was fast becoming intimate, when at once the whole tenor and complexion of the voyage was changed.

They were entering that dreadful bay of St. Andrew's! Logan, who was unaware of its ill name, had just commenced a dissertation to his new friend on the ancient seat of Scottish learning, when, in the first place, the sight of a man in sailor's clothes, bearing a marvellous resemblance to Fletcher (Effie's friend's brother), whom he believed at that moment to be in Jamaica, threw him out of his discourse, and the rather that the man seemed to avoid his eye, skulking away the moment he saw him among the steerage passengers forward;* and in the next place, ere he had well time to reflect on this incident, he was arrested by a change of motion in the vessel itself, and his whole soul (so to speak) curdled up in the unaccountable phenomena. There was no apparent wind. Merciful Providence! was the steamer pos-

---

* It seems not improbable, as the reader will see a few chapters hence, that this may have been Fletcher himself. I make the interesting note from the fact that Mr. Gideon was an old flame of Effie's, and his supposed reappearance here in sailor's clothes is quite in the romantic school.

sessed—was she going down ? His new acquaintance, a grave sort of person, assured
him it was nothing : " She was a first-rate
sea poat, and only making a little harm-
less sport, goot lass, with the old saint in his
bay, what the crew called tumbling her
lundies ; but young beginners would be at
the bucket their first voyage, and their
betterest in that case was to go below."
The advice of this northern oracle, though
rather obscurely worded, seemed not un-
sound, and accordingly our envoy disap-
pears for a season.

Effie stood it out bravely ; she escaped
with a little miff, not very urgent, just as
they were swirling round the farther horn
of the bay and regaining still water. After
that succeeded a long delicious reverie, of
which every one on deck seemed to partici-
pate less or more as they steamed away
before the strong September sun. It was,

of course, harvest time, and Effie, who liked to sail as near the land as possible, enjoyed it most when she could make out the faces of the "shearers" as they stood at gaze admiring the splendid new creature of the deep. And then would come stripes of solitary green, old pasture braes, with only a narrow fringe of grey shore, on which for miles no sign of man or human habitation was to be seen.

A passenger walking the deck by himself, who had much the air of a gentleman, observing that Effie was a young traveller, and apparently alone, paid her some attention: he told her the names of places, villages, towns, when they occurred, country seats, manses, kirks, remarkable headlands, old castles, hills in the distance. He spoke with the tongue of a proprietor, and was obviously far above Effie in station, yet was his voice pleasant in Effie's ear. And but for this same attentive gentleman (though he looked as proud and absent at times as Lucifer) our poor pilgrim would have dined but sparingly, that is to say, got no dinner at all. He brought her, before sitting down to table himself, some sandwich and a glass of sherry, which, between ourselves, when the donor was gone, Effie enjoyed very much, regretting only that Logan was not by to share; but the envoy was still afraid to re-venture upon deck in case of a relapse.

Before evening of the first day's sail the company was somewhat thinned by dis-embarkations along the coast. Most of the ladies had gone below for the night; a few, however, still remained, and the gen-tlemen were smoking their cigars in ani-mated discussion; among them Effie's friend. (" How handsome and clever he

is!" thought Effie; "he must be something
more or less than a mere proprietor.")
The shore, though near, was gradually
growing dimmer with the advance of evening, and there was a small, delicious Sep-
tembral chill blowing off the land. The
steamer was going on as swift and as steady
and still as a humming-top asleep. And our
hero, tempted by the stillness of the hour
and the smooth water, without current or
wimple, prevailing under the shadow of
the land, came again upon deck.

Among the few Logan made acquaintance with we were about to notice one in
particular—the *fidus Achates* of the voyage
—when we were interrupted in St. Andrew's Bay. Effie could not conceive what
attracted her brother to this man, unless
it were his uncouth and most extraordinary personal appearance and dress.
He was coarsely clad in the extreme of

the tourist mode, with an eye, apparently, to make a youthful appearance, but he was obviously rather ancient; moreover, he was more robust than buck beseems; and he wore the beard, a yellow one, like Hudibras's, of which it was impossible to conjecture whether he was proud or ashamed, as, despite his singularities of outward man, he looked melancholy and depressed, at times unconsciously so, as if the grisly ornament had been imposed upon him by way of penance. In a word, there was an expression of solicitude about the man's face that would have defied a physiognomist to say whether he wished or did not wish to draw the gazer's eye.

Curious to know what so odd a wight could have to say, Effie endeavoured to pick up something of their conversation as they passed and repassed her, pacing the deck. And first, it was evident they were

in close confab about nothing—Beardie's
part in the dialogue being quite up to his
tout ensemble. He spoke the high English of the insular north—that is to say,
with the assumption of a person of consideration, but whose schooling in early
youth had, from some unlucky cause, been
neglected. The blunders he made were
painful, and, what made it worse, the poor
man himself seemed to be haunted by a
vague suspicion of his deficiency and the
hope of its passing unnoticed. "Some
country schoolmaster returning home from
the vacation," thought Effie. "I am so
glad to see Logan paying the poor thing a
little attention;" and probably such would
have been the general impression from the
man's high English.

Why, you simple Effie! Are you aware
that this supposed pedagogue from the far
north is the descendant of a long line of

Norse heroes ages ago extinct, laird in his own person of an independent island still, and, what is more, destined, at no very distant date, to come down in that most modern form of the *deus ex machinâ*, a suitor to yourself. Well prophesied your poor old friend Mr. John Davidson.

Something in the above style would have been the fraternal correction of Effie's mistake had Logan been aware of it; but, to do him justice, he was not in the least aware of the weight of his new acquaintance. He never thought of asking himself what the man was. His mission concerned men, not what were they. Humanity, then, and a touch, perhaps, of fellow feeling, made up his whole motive: it struck him there was an objection to the poor man on account of his yellow beard, just as some fastidious people objected to the length of his own chin ; he seemed to be generally avoided; and this it was which induced Logan to make up to the hirsute solitary. Beardie was abundantly grateful for the notice, and in return gave his reverend young acquaintance to know that he was in company of Mr. Balph Ruddock, of Fair Hall, in Venturefair, a fact which Mr. Ruddock assured Logan was perfectly well known on board, notwithstanding the general appearance to the contrary. " I come of the old stock, sir," said Mr. Ruddock; "and it seems to be a part of their college-bred learning and modern airs and graces now-a-days, to prefer the breeding to the breed." Was this a witticism? Logan was certainly startled.

Your neglected man is done for the moment he opens his mouth to complain; from that moment our envoy's eyes were opened : he discovered that Mr. Ruddock, poor man, was a very tiresome twaddler, one of those dreary talking, endless wights, shut up, as it were, and tormented for ever in their own obscurity, whose conversation the light of meaning never visits, and from whom it is hopeless to think of extracting the commonest piece of information relative to what is going on about them. When asked about the Hallow family, although he was their next-door neighbour, his budget amounted to this : " Oh—ah— yes—in a way, in a way; a very nice family by this time I doan't doubt—and as the crow flies good company—at home they doan't somehow know people. We heard the owd man's dying, but I couldn't just say for certain — he's a very owd man whatever — twenty years, I should say, owder than she is—and that's just the tangle, that's where the downdie is, bless you, ay!" This profound piece of social criticism can only be explained in a note.*

But it was weeks, some two or three afterwards, before Logan discovered that this Orcadian Solomon, on whose very vitals an incurable melancholy was preying, had nevertheless considerable pretensions to be thought a wit : it was only when he made the acquaintance of his brother, Mr. Petrie Ruddock, that that gentleman let the cat out of the bag—it was a family one—the Ruddocks were all wits. On the great question of the day it is scarcely necessary

* In case any reader should have the curiosity to see Mr. Ruddock's joke interpreted, *downdie* is the name given in Orkney to a kind of sickly cod that haunts the tangle or seaware in-shore, until it becomes more and more wormeaten and dies. Hence the dying laird twenty years older (owder) than his wife seems to have struck Mr. Balph's dreary imagination in the light of a downdie.

to add here that poor Mr. Ruddock was deplorably ignorant, though in his way a sort of well-wisher. He seemed a pious man, but his piety appeared to be that of a hermit disappointed in the world, and aspiring only to bread-and-water and a cell.

These are all the particulars, and I hope I have not been tedious in the account of this voyage. It seldom happens that the second day's sail is equal to the first: the weather, ten to one, is not so fine; but at any rate, in the case of persons unused to sea travelling, there comes a lassitude both of body and mind after the first fresh impression wears off. Passing John o'Groat's and the Land's-end, nothing more was for some time to be seen; all was blank; a cold mist concealed the Orkneys. Our young travellers were, therefore, upon the whole, glad when the steamer arrived in the roadstead at Kirkwal. And yet it came, as it were, suddenly. How our envoy was stunned by the booming complicated roar called by the stokers and other ministering gnomes of the engine-room " letting off the steam !"

CHAPTER V.

THEY LAND AT KIRKWAL — INTERVIEW WITH A WEALTHY
KIRKWAL MERCHANT—LOGAN'S FIRST IMPRESSIONS OF THE
ORCADIAN METROPOLIS NOT FAVOURABLE.

THE happiness attending the conclusion
of a voyage differs from that of its commencement in nothing so much as in the
matter of seeing to the luggage. Then it
is that a poor stranger (unless he be an old
hand) has no chance with the natives, and
must undergo with what patience he may
the misery and delay of getting at his own
in the horrid selfish scuffle.

Our envoy was no exception to the common lot. With the anxious Effie looking on and assisting him, Logan was made to feel his situation acutely, ere, with his baggage collected on the quay of Kirkwal, he was at leisure to look around him and ask whither next? For further direction in the prosecution of his voyage, he was referred to a Mr. Duncan Rapness, a shopkeeper of some note, to whom he had a letter of introduction from Bland. Having with some difficulty, and the loss of an old hat-case, got his chattels to the inn, it was not so difficult to find out Mr. Rapness.

He found Mr. Duncan Rapness in his shop—or rather store, for it appeared to be an omnium gatherum of every species of merchandise—an elderly man of slow and serious deportment of the Daidle type, but not so clerical, not nearly so prepossessing in his appearance as the worthy bibliopolist of —— street. He was a short, corpulent

man, with a mellow·face, but a severe eye,
an elder in the United Secession Church,
and worth twenty thousand pounds —
rather a trying judge of our friend's pretensions and mission.   Moreover, Mr.
Duncan Rapness had a fashionable wife,
and was to some extent himself a man of
society.

The look with which he took the letter
of introduction was quite enough for Logan;
had that been insufficient, the cough that
called attention to his reading it, would
have more than filled up the measure of
our hero's opinion of Mr. Duncan Rapness.
So easy is it from the merest trifles to conceive a prejudice.   " I could tell from that
man's talk," said Logan, " that he was
bred to filling barrels !"   This, you must
know, was in reference to the outpouring
of Mr. Duncan's reception of our hero.

" You have just arrived, sir, I find, from

my friend Mr. Bland. And how is Mr. B.—
well, I hope? And you have had a comfortable passage, of course? Kith, run
down to your father, and ask him when
the *Tom Tub* sails. That's the family mar-
ket-boat, sir, I am requested to see you
forwarded by; she came in for provisions
this morning. Skeely!"(addressing another
lint-topped youngster), " what are you
standing gaping at there, doing nothing?
See what that wean's wanting. These are
serious times, Mr. Macmorlan; it must be
owned there was great need for such a lift
among you. I hope and trust it will pro-
sper; and that now, having left the flesh-
pots of Egypt, you will by-and-by be all of
one accord and mind to cast your spoons
and fling the ladle behind you also."

" If you refer, sir," interposed Logan,
" to our unsettled claims upon the
State——"

" By no means," continued Mr. Duncan
Rapness. "There will, doubtless, be the
proper referees, whose business it is. I
was merely going to say, that so report and
the newspapers speak of you."

A young lady of fashionable appearance
entered the shop.

" How do you do, Miss Rachel, and how
is mamma ? None the worse for being at
the concert the other night, I hope ? I
observed that she had a slight thoughty of
a cold. This is Mr. Macmorlan, of the new
station at Hallow, Miss Rachel." (A gra-
ciously stiff bow from Miss Rachel.) " I
thought I saw some of the young gentlemen in town to-day," &c. &c.

Between them, they kept him waiting a
full quarter of an hour, until he was quite
sick at heart of their idle talk. Logan
thought the girl's vanity bad enough, but
the old parasite was intolerable. At length,

with a gracious good-day to Mr. Rapness, a rather stinted inclination to our friend, and a sharp glance at Effie, who was standing in the doorway, the Orcadian damsel left the shop.

The sequel was a little more palatable.

"One of our Kirkwal young ladies; a great belle, sir, I assure you; much run after; indeed, word goes that the Master of Hallow and Miss Rachel Shore are, or if not just yet, *about to be;* in respect of which report, there are others, again, who think the Master is not a person to pauge with" ("pauge," tamper with). "But these are all matters by the way to you, sir, as yet. Skeely, run down and see what's keeping Kith. As I said before, Mr. Macmorlan, you have my best wishes, and I hope soon to hear of your usefulness out-by."

"And now, sir," said Logan, "may I

request the favour of a little private conversation with you?"

Mr. Duncan Rapness looked a little surprised at the request, but motioning him
to follow, he led the way into his private
counting-room behind the shop; whither
we need not accompany them, as Mr. Rapness was extremely cautious in his replies,
and nothing of any importance was elicited
by the queries which Logan deemed it incumbent upon him to put, just to let Mr.
Duncan Rapness know who he was.

" Effie," said Logan, as he passed her on
his way to the inner shrine of Mammon, " I
shall probably be half an hour here yet;
you had better, dear, go and see the cathedral and amuse yourself, but don't go
far away."

So Effie went and saw the cathedral.
The day was such as to show it to advantage: it was windy and cloudy, but with

abundance of flying sunshine between showers. The cathedral—first, greatest, and most imposing sight—what a vision it was! A wavering mass of sunshine and gloom, wavering upward from the ground! All seemed straining, and as it were in motion, from the massive pillars of the lofty interior seen flashing through the windows between the buttresses of solid masonry, to the battlement of the tower and to the creaking cock on the spire!

As Effie stood and listened to the booming of the huge edifice, thoughts of Glasgow Minster and its associations crowded on her mind, and she said, as the tears flowed down her cheeks, " If there was a bit running water of ony kind that ane could tak for the Molindinar Burn, and if that street was only langer and higher, it might pass for the Saltmarket !"

To spare the purse, she had taken no breakfast that morning, and it was now three in the afternoon. Hungry and anxious, and really very temptingly pretty, more than one of the Kirkwal youths wondered who the deuce she was.

On her return, Mr. Rapness, without his hat, and his pen behind his ear, was bowing Logan off the premises. So much for the letter of introduction.

Thanking the old shopkeeper for his good wishes, he repaired, under guidance of a young counter-jumper, to the little half-decked vessel in which the remainder of his journey was to be performed. And here he was still further shocked at the ignorance and indifference of the people; when informed who he was, and desired to see about getting his luggage down from the hotel, the boatmen absolutely refused to obey the word of command, and in a dialect or idiom the most uncouth conceivable.

"Nyah! they dreedna do that—they had orders on na account to grund." (They had orders not to let the vessel ground.) And when asked when they were to sail, "It would be a peri while yet." What a peri while might be, Logan, of course, could not conjecture, nor did it much matter, as their hyperborean notions of a little while would probably have differed considerably from his. Peri is a word of frequent occurrence in the Orkney dialect, and means "little." Altogether, his reception began to put our envoy out of temper.

"Look ye, my men," said he, "I have told you that I am a clergyman, but it would appear that you do not know what that is; when I add that I am the bearer of letters to Mrs. Deerness, does it not occur to you as possible that you may rue this yet?"

The menace had some effect. The men began to converse in whispers, directing an occasional furtive glance at their pale and peremptory passenger.

"What think, men?" said he who was called Captain Kith. "Foroddin, sirs, if I like's looks!* There is a sough out-by amang the quinies (young women) about the Ald Woman and this new evangel; if this should be the who-ca'd that they say she's expecting, it's like to skirl up a blast about our lugs—the kelp kilns drowned out will be nothing til't. Dreed and keep us in that terrible day o' the Ald Woman! Annie Gate'us (Gatehouse) tell'd my wife."

" Also and for certain," observed another

---

* Foroddin—probably Fore Odin, and equivalent to our English Fore God. I don't think the expression is common, having never heard it used except by Captain Kith.

old fellow, who answered to the name of Hoolie, "the said Annie Gate'us tell'd mine that the last preachin' ald Crawtaes was across she forbad him the grund—warned him aff—the like sic a carfuffle between the twa was never heard. But the laird he said nou't."

"Ye hear that—ye hear what Hoolie says?" resumed Captain Kith. "I wad now there was a man of some lair amang us, for it fickles me what to do. What say, Smith? You are a man that deals in hammerin' het iron cald—what say?"

"Calm ye, Kith, I'm nae the fule," replied the Vulcan of Hallow. "I say as the laird says, nou't; only this here, let me out-by, and I ken fase door will be new shod furthwith."*

---

* The horse-shoe nailed on the door, originally against witchcraft, and latterly as a prevention of calamity generally, is still practised in these islands.

" You hear, men and boys," said Captain
Kith, " an it be come so near the doors as
that we maun all have our shoes turned.
Hoolie, man, gang up to Mother Shore's
(Miss Rachel's mamma) and ask a word
o' Mr. Weatherby."

" The ne'er a fut o' me," said Hoolie.
" An there maun be a fule amang us, gang
yoursel', Kith."

Hoolie's reputation as an oracle and de-
liverer of dark sayings was high. Distinguished even in early youth for his sombre
parts, he had stood the blast of some fifty
winters, predicted disease among cattle and
geese, and foundered many a goodly boat,
so that Captain Kith was really very much
perplexed how to act. On the whole, however, the fear of the unknown prevailed,
and he stepped on shore, intimating by
a mute signal to Logan to follow him.

Following his guide up the town, and being desired to wait at the corner of the street, he saw the skipper at the door of a house in the west end, apparently stating the case to a fashionably dressed young man, whose appearance reminded him vastly of the youth of Princes-street. Presently the fellow returned, and said: " It was all right now; they had Mr. Weatherby's orders to tak 's luggage on board, and tell the gentleman they were not to sail before seven o'clock, whatever later."

" Stay," said Logan ; " I have a question to ask you, Mr. Captain. Do you mean to tell me, my good fellow, that you seriously thought me not admissible to an audience with this Mr. Weatherby, a younger brother ?"

But the captain did not understand the words of action. He made a motion, how-

ever, of humbling himself, and chattered
out something that sounded like begging
pardon.

The interval he spent in visiting the
ruins of the palaces and the old cathedral
of St. Magnus. Effie was again much impressed with the latter, but Logan was
disappointed; it was too large for the place.
How came it there at all? There was
an almost antediluvian look about it; the
expression was painful; it reminded him of
some vast and crumbling image of dust
that would be far better away. His business there was with the living pomps and
vanities, not with the architectural mum-
meries of a bygone age.

It was not the cathedral alone—he was
disappointed altogether. At every step it
was becoming more and more apparent that
Orkney was not the field he took it for;
that, opposed to the ignorance of the

common people, it had its gentry, its capital, and a society and civilisation of its
own ; and to Morland, whose virtues inclined a little to the morose side at any
rate, such discoveries were especially un-
palatable after the tossing of a sea voyage.
He had no patience with the amount of
dandyism they encountered. " Did you
ever," said he, " see such puppies ?"

" Where ?" said Effie. " Oh ! these
young men away past. What's the matter
with them ?"

" I mean to say," continued the angry
envoy, "that Princes-street airs are su-
premely ridiculous here, and the swell out
of all proportion to the narrowness of the
streets. Streets ! Why they are hardly
even lanes, appearing not to have been
laid down to any plan, but to have been
picked out afterwards as chance or caprice
directed."

" It was a pity," Effie said, " that they
had not thought of making them a little
wider."

" I am not complaining of the streets,
you simpleton, but of the discrepancy between them and the people! The frivo-
lities of fashion are insufferable enough
anywhere, but to meet with such antics
here, it is an insult to all the dead Picts,
more properly Peghs, whose habitations
are said to abound in these islands. Did
you remark that great lump of a girl who
came into what's his name's shop when I
was there ?"

" She was rather tall if anything, but
otherwise not bad-looking, I thought."

" Pshaw! I tell you," said the envoy,
" if ever I saw folly in the flesh it was
that gawk. Dido was nothing to her !"

Most welcome was the change to our
weary Effie when, after wandering about

the whole chill afternoon, and a so-so dinner at the inn embittered by the envoy's grumblings, evening at length brought the hour to sail.

It appeared they were going to have some fellow - passengers. There were about half a dozen poor people belonging to Hallow on board, and Captain Kith, ready to put to sea, was waiting for the young gentlemen. Five — ten minutes, and no appearance of them. Night, mean: while, closed round, and our envoy took his seat. From the sound of the wind in the vessel's rigging he began to have some not over-pleasant anticipations of what it would be out at sea, and he said to himself, "How would Bland, if he were in my shoes, like this?"

A gentleman stepped on board.

"Are not these boys come yet? Peter Dreaver, go up and tell them that if they do not come immediately we sail without them." It was the Master. His tone struck Logan as peremptory.

"Fusht! I think I hear them coming," said the captain, who had a long ear to the convivial; and down they came, great, blooming, boisterous youths, and all very merry. They sprang into the half-deck, where, according to custom, they fell in a body upon Captain Kith and half worried him. This performance ended, they lit up their pipes, sitting like ducks in a row on the half-deck rail, while the captain, a special favourite, as appeared from this rough caress, set about his work. The sails were hoisted, and they slipped out of the harbour and across the bay of Kirkwal before a light breeze—so light, indeed, that it took my friend by surprise; but he was impatient, off his proper poise, and every way in the exaggerating mood.

Effie would have thought the vessel quite stationary, from the gurgling under-sound of the water, had not the diminishing lights of Kirkwal assured her that they were already some distance on their watery way; and by-and-by their progress became more distinctly traceable as they glided close in shore past a large low-lying island. Effie had no doubt it must be beautifully green, from the dewy fragrance of the grass. At times she fancied she could have put out her hand and touched the margin, but they were not so very near as she imagined, and in a little it faded and disappeared.

CHAPTER VI.

SAILING FOR HALLOW THEY ARE BENIGHTED IN OYSTER
SOUND.

An hour—they could hear it strike from
the distant steeple of St. Magnus—and
not a word addressed to him by the Master.
As for the younger lads, sitting smoking
forward, they kept up an incessant chatter
with Captain Kith, but the precise subject
of their conversation my friend could not
make out.   Logan began to think it high
time to pluck up his clerical character,

and accordingly he set off with an observation on the weather.

"I am afraid sir," said he, addressing the principal person on board, "we are going to have a tedious passage to-night."

"It looks like it," he replied, in a tone of civil indifference (Effie thought she had heard the voice before); and then added, addressing Captain Kith, who was at the helm, "Where is the wind to-night, Kith —on the land or on the water?"

"I'm doubtin' she's on the land," replied the captain; "will we shaw her the oar, sir?"

The Orkney boatmen abound in these quaint allegorical phrases, remnants, no doubt, of the old Scandinavian mythology. This of showing the oar is a favourite and frequent, for, though a boisterous climate, it is extremely variable, and they are as subject to calms as to storms. It means, in plain terms, holding up the oar and threatening to pull if the lubber wind won't get up.

" Look at the light through Blower-ness," said the Master, still addressing Captain Kith; " I rather think she's bedded on the water to-night. I expect a puff when we get a little further out."

" If I was to gie my opinion," said the old man whom they called Hoolie, " I wad be mair fearder we'se gan to get a blash o' rain."

" The devil, Hoolie! what puts rain in your head ?"

" I kenna, sir," replied Hoolie, " but I'm amaist for certain we'se gan to get a blash o' something ere lang."

" Do you see any appearance of rain, sir ?" inquired Logan.

" Not the least," he replied; " but we are sure to have rain if Hoolie says it. He sleeps a good deal, and hears at a great distance in his sleep. His brain seems to be a kind of fungus, and to require rain, and he is always sure to awaken before it comes on."

Logan was at a loss to determine whether he was bantering him or gravely describing Hoolie as a natural curiosity. "Are we far yet from Hallow?" he inquired; and this, still politely enough, was answered by the counter-question,

" Are you going, sir, to Hallow?"

" I believe I am, sir, going there (he-he-hem !)," replied my friend, a little nettled at his own hesitation, and his being forced to disguise it under that parenthetical cough.

The Master was silent for about half a minute; at length he spoke:

" May I take the liberty, sir, to ask your name?"

"Morland—the Reverend Logan Morland."

"Of the Free Church," said the Master, and was again silent.

"You are acquainted with the name of Bland, sir, I think?" suggested Logan.

"Look out forward there; is that wind coming?"

"There's something coming," returned his brethren, with a grunting laugh; and Logan followed to the fore-deck rail, where they all stood listening.

"The rain's on!" roared Captain Kith from the stern-sheets.

"I tald ye sae," quoth Hoolie.

And down it poured in torrents. In the bustle and tumbling about that followed, the envoy had perforce to sit mute.

It was now resolved, with all hands at the oars, to make for the nearest island of Scapaway, but in the darkness accompanying the rain, the question was which way to pull for it. At length, after groping about for nearly half an hour, Captain Kith's oar brought up a tangle; and at the same moment a stentorian voice shouted from the shore, "Is that you, Melethor?"

"It's Markus!" cried the younger lads; "whatever in all the world can he be doing there!" The question being put by the Master to the party on shore, it was immediately answered by an overture on the bagpipes so uncouth, loud and louder swelling, as if it would rend the very darkness, that our envoy, in the strangeness of the scene, could have almost fancied for a moment that the piper must be Satan himself.

"I ken fat it's like now," observed Captain Kith; "we'll be in Oyster Sound, at Mr. Skeldar's new oyster-beds, and that's

himsel'; he'll hae gard big a hoos ye'll
find." The pibroch ceased, and the piper,
again uplifting his voice, shouted, " Here's
to you all ! aren't you coming ashore ?"
The invitation was accepted in a similar
strain with a volley of laughter; they ran
the yacht in, and the young men having
disembarked, the little vessel was again
pulled out of grounding as the tide was
ebb, and anchored in six fathoms water,
about half a stone's cast from the beach.

It was still raining heavily, but not
quite so dark. Effie could just dimly see
the beach. And now Captain Kith, the gentlemen having gone to royster it on shore
with the enterprising projector of the new
oyster-beds, proceeded in like manner to
make as merry and comfortable as things
admitted of on board. Having cleared
the hold under the half-deck of a portion
of its miscellaneous cargo, he stowed in

all the poor people; then, with the aid of
a spirit-lamp which the young men always
took care to carry with them on their
voyages, he converted a pan of water into
good hot punch; and finally, in as cour-
teous phrase as he could muster, he invited the envoy to partake.

There is nothing like a good sound
ducking to make a man succumb to the
creature comforts of food, drink, and shel-
ter, in however humble a guise presented;
and our friend, though a little disgusted at
not having been asked on shore, made no
scruple to accept of the captain's hospitality.

At this symposium, Effie behaving with
a cheerfulness that won the hearts of
the boatmen, drank their healths in a
moderate sip of the can, to the infinite
admiration of old Hoolie, who scratched
his weather-gage, *i. e.* his head, and ob-

served that he thought "it was gan to fair."

" Here's til her ! she's a brave lass whatever," said Captain Kith, staring with might and main at his compeers.

Logan, too, made an attempt to enter into the humour of his whimsical situation, but failed—chiefly from their excessive use of new or obsolete words ; these were constantly throwing gaps in his way, which took him so long to get over, that in a very little time he found himself involved in a conversation that, with lights of meaning here and there, felt, the further he proceeded, like a gloomy and interminable morass ; and this was the more annoying, as, in the main, their dialect, though spoken with an odd twang, appeared to be intelligible enough. Thus the night wore away, the boatmen telling long, dreary stories about nothing, and the

envoy making desperate efforts to get a
little sleep. He succeeded at last.

" The rain's ower," said Hoolie; and he
fell asleep too.

Effie had no inclination to sleep; she
crept out, and, wrapping herself in a boat-
cloak, sat down to wait for morning. All
was silent—the sweet and solemn silence
after the rain. Captain Kith and his
crew, poor souls, were all asleep over their
empty can, but occasionally a wild burst
of revelry fell upon the water from the
party who were keeping it up on shore.
These convivial shells ceased in their turn,
and Effie was left to herself. At length
she fell into a kind of trance, feeling con-
scious that she was awake, but all the while
dreaming as much and as fast as if she had
been asleep. In vain she endeavoured to
take a steady review of their Orkney prospects. Fancy her dismay, when looking

forward to see Logan useful and respected
at his own fireside, she saw him carica-
tured in a manner the most ridiculous
and irreverend, put up in such a tableau
vivant as this : throned, and holding forth
to the drinking party on shore at Mr.
Skeldar's, with the bagpipes at his feet,
uttering ever and anon of their own accord a wild expiring drone, which, being
interpreted, was understood to mean the
image of Satan under foot; presently, to
this succeeded a dance on the top of
the table, the pipes playing of their
own accord, and who lighter of foot than
her brother Logan, who was no dancer,
and highly disapproved of the practice?
But the last was the severest, for lo ! a
hand was stretched over the revellers—a
well-remembered hand (old Sanders's of
the Salt-market)—and Logan was igno-
miniously carried off and laid down on his

bed at home. He was very ill; Sanders said it was the measles, and Effie was set to watch by the bedside just as she had done when they were children. And so on until daybreak awoke her.

She was not at first very sure whether the tremulous motion on the water was really the dawn, or merely some trick of the night; by-and-by, however, objects became more distinct, and the clouds moving about in their grey and proper forms assured Effie it was morning.

Oyster Sound is one of the finest points in the Orcadian archipelago. Land-locked all round, it has the appearance of a, secluded lake; and to Effie Morland these solitary green islands, as she beheld them in the dawn of morning, with their handful of poor houses, some with none, and apparently uninhabited, presented a scene as novel as it was affecting. Beauty is al-

ways more difficult to analyse in proportion as it recedes from its compound to its
simpler forms. We see situations apparently with scarcely a single attraction,
according to our established notions of
fine scenery, which yet subdue us in a
manner that we never felt before the
finest celebrities of the grand route.

On the other hand, Logan's first impression was more complex, not nearly so
natural, and perhaps what now befel him
had some antagonistic affinity with the
preceding dream of his sister. The same
scene that Effie beheld with her waking
eyes was presented to his slumbering sense.
He beheld in a dream these same green
islands from shore to summit literally
covered with a swarm of the ancient Pict-
ish aborigines, like so many imps broken
loose from the pit of darkness, every one
more eager than another to get at him,

making faces at him, mocking his person and his mission. One put out his leg, and grew by that member till he almost touched the slumberer, but, stepping short, fell into the sea; another grew by the chin, holding up a looking-glass; another, by the nose: across the water it shot, nearer and nearer, tipped with two fiery, prying eyes—preposterous sight! Logan started back in affright, and awoke.

Considered in reference to his prospects, this vision troubled him very much at the time, but in his subsequent interpretation it was made all right to him. In the first place, there would be no end to the ignorance and opposition he might expect to encounter; still it would be all of a petty kind. The leg was obviously indicative of some faction destined to come to nothing— to fall into the sea. The chin, it was pretty plain to what that pointed; were Adonis himself to reappear in orders, there would be women and fools enough to spy faults. The nose, there could be as little doubt about that—*that* was typical of the old Residuary who predominated in the neighbouring isle; his jurisdiction extended to Hallow, and it was hardly to be expected that courtesy would prevent him from taking an occasional sniff at the new pastor and his proceedings.

But all this was the fruit of after study; and starting up from his dream, cold, scared, and hardly knowing where he was, in the grey dead of the morning, Logan, it may be supposed, was not in the mood to approve of Effie's happy face.

"You seem vastly pleased with the politeness of these people," he observed. Effie was intent upon the nearest white strip of sand—there were foot-prints on it sufficient to indicate it as the landing-

place of the preceding night. " My estimate of them is somewhat different from
yours; I would not have you think me
carping, Effie, but I must say it, I begin
to despair of your spiritual insight—you
are far too much taken up with these
youths——"

" I was only thinking of that funny
man, the captain," said Effie; which, indeed, was the case.

" To the neglect, I was about to say,"
continued Logan, " of higher considerations. *I* am captain here. The report of
the night I have passed will rather asto-
nish them at head-quarters, I fancy. In the
mean time, are we ever to get out of this, I
wonder ? If these bacchanals do not make
their appearance very soon, I shall certainly order the men to sail without them."
The latter sentence he pronounced with
marked emphasis, looking his sister stea-

dily in the face, to see whether she would dare to smile. Far from smiling, the true-hearted, simple Effie pleaded with him as if he had had no more ado than to give the word : " For mercy's sake, do not, brother! it would be sure to give offence, and might lead to no end of quarrels." And Logan turned away with an internal chuckle, satisfied that his power to influence ("to will and to do," was his favourite phrase) was not altogether a myth.

Effie was not quite so sure about Mr. Skeldar, or that she could entirely approve of the young men's intimacy with that gentleman; they were fine, handsome young fellows, she knew by their laugh, whereas he must be pot-bellied and red-nosed, and it was a pity they should devote themselves to such a leader. That never-to-be-forgotten prelude on the bagpipes seemed to argue a debauch a little too much after the ancient Norse fashion, when the men were all most foaming drinkers; but as the thing was in a measure, accidental, it was to be hoped such orgies were not of frequent occurrence: most probably it was his house-heating— the boatmen seemed to speak of his having been building lately. Accordingly, as the morning clouds rolled away from off the nearer island, Effie expected every moment they would disclose a handsome new mansion, or if not that, an old one, to justify her charitable conjectures. But no such house appeared; all was one solitary mass of green, the craggy summits still seething in the morning mist, and as far as the eye could reach not a vestige of human habitation was to be seen, with the exception of a shingle shed appearing over the neighbouring point that formed the termination of the small slip of sandy beach off which they lay anchored.

That same shingle shed, such as it was, had the honour to be the seat, for the present, of the wandering and eccentric Markus Skeldar of Long-annot.

About seven o'clock, Captain Kith got ready some breakfast—coffee and bread— which he served out to the poorer passengers first; he apologised to the Morlands for having nothing better to offer them, and chiefly and especially for his having no butter, which Captain Kith esteemed the greatest luxury and prime lubricator of life; and truly so it is when folks have to eat oaten cakes six days out of the seven. The captain observed " that there was a grand cabin in the Master's own yacht, and *plenty of butter and every-*

thing, but the *Tom Tub* was just the provision boat for gan to market in," &c.

Effie, having finished her coffee, looked again to the slip of sand; two men were walking on its grassy margin. In the almost gigantic figure of one she had no doubt that she beheld Mr. Skeldar; in the other she recognised not only the Master of Hallow, but by a smart, peculiar kind of grace in his walk, her civil friend on board the steamer, who told her the names of the places along the coast.

The envoy also perceiving them, in an instant he was at his sister's side. He stared angrily for nearly a minute at the two gentlemen, and then said, "They take it coolly, I must say! They appear to be in close conversation; what on earth can they find here of so very absorbing a nature?" Effie made no reply; instinctively she felt that they themselves were the subject of conversation, and that the conversation was serious.

It is rather a stale story-teller's trick, but we must e'en put up with it; let us hear what the Master and Mr. Skeldar are saying.

" But I say, Melethor," quoth Markus, who was some nine-and-twenty or thirty, and four or five years the Master's senior, "how comes this to put up your back so ? you were used to be reckoned a cool enough hand at the pretensions of haly kirk."

" So far as I myself am concerned," replied the Master, " I might manage to make shift and even to hold my tongue, but that is not the question. Take it home to yourself, Markus, my boy! You like your smoke, you like your beer, you like to come to Hallow, and you cannot budge a foot without the pipes. Very well. Suppose this reverend new comer should take it into his head to say to you some day, ' Give me that noisy anti-christian bag of wind till I put my foot in it, you cannot be allowed to make a noise with it here; your pipe and your tobacco-box, smoking is not allowed; your solemn vow not to drink, to learn your catechism, say your prayers, and go to bed sober—it is a shame to see such a great fat man.' How do you think would our stout friend relish such a proposal?"

" Oh, bosh !" returned Markus Skeldar, " the beggar can't be so bad as all that. Why, in the old time of the Rump they never turned out a fellow to such an extent as that. Give up the pipes ! Stop my grog !"

" Yes, strip you of pipes and everything, and leave you without a sin to your back, man ! I don't say that this lad, though I won't warrant him, would actually have the hardihood to address you in such terms to your face, but don't you see, if my mother takes on with these people (and I am afraid she will), then everything I have said follows as a matter of course, and we will precious seldom see Markus Skeldar at Hallow after that."

"But what the deil are they, man, these people?" cried Markus, in considerable perplexity; "they must surely be a stiff sect to take up ground like that. But one thing is clear, they'll never do for Orkney! Is there no possibility of keeping them out? Why let them get footing at all? Will not your father interfere?"

"Alas! no, Markus. My father, I doubt, will soon be where it is all over both with sects and sinners," said the Master, sorrowfully.

" Is he so ill ?" inquired Skeldar. " He's not been worse, has he ?"

" No, not particularly worse, but the old man's wearing away."

" Well," observed his friend, after a thoughtful pause, " the blast that bears the news that auld Hallow is gane ʿwill gie a shake to maist of the ingles in Orkney !"

" It will, Markus," said the Master. " My father is a good old man. I wish I were like him."

There was another short pause, which Markus Skeldar devoted to reflection. Eyeing his companion askance,

" Curse me," thought the burly Norseman, "if he is not going to catch the infection himself! he'll be as mad as his mother before all's done with this same new reformation." He resumed their conversation. "But you have not told me your news from the south yet; I suppose this new light is making a mighty stir down thereaway ?"

"Pho! you don't suppose I went to Edinburgh about that? I had something else to look after. I have got my father's settlements revised; Rollockson says they are all right. He's to be down as soon as the court rises. As to this new light, as you call it, the men, I suppose, are in earnest, and as far as I understand their quarrel, it seems a perfectly fair one; what I resent is their cool assurance in clapping themselves down here. In the first place, I cannot very well see what motive they can have for it; and in the next, I can see most clearly it is to be productive of family quarrels, not to mention a daily theological addition to all that vulgar bickering which I detest. Jerrold, if you noticed, has caught some of the slang already, and seems more than half disposed to enter the lists as their bottle-holder."

"So I noticed," said Skeldar, "but he was very groggy, and he'll come round again. A thought strikes me. How would it do to clap their missionary in limbo for a while? they'll think he has been drowned on the passage, or run away, and so may not be at the trouble to send another. I'll undertake to keep him here in Craigery, where never man will hear the cheep of him till he has the sense to turn his neb anither gate."

The other, with equal gravity, replied : "I had some thought of that myself, but kidnapping's rather a dangerous thing to try ; and besides, he is not alone, there's a young woman with him—

his wife or sister—a pretty, modest-looking girl enough; and so you see I couldn't think of using the poor things so. They have come a long way, and I dare say the young chap (for he's but a lad) thinks it's for our good, for so think they all."

" Young is he? Upon my soul, it's too bad! But you say he's young? In that case, and if he has the sense to be guided by them that ken where the best pasture lies, the case may not be so bad after all."

" And Markus Skeldar come off with flying pipes and all the rest of it! Dream not of it, my dear Mark. We have brought this upon ourselves: I told old Calthrop and Caldwel Gilchrist as much years ago. I wonder what my reverend cousin Caldwel will say to it now—the man whom the women call perfect, the courtier and the Christian, who would not stoop to do a mean thing—nor a useful thing either—the dignified, do-nothing, proud Churchman! Well, for the pleasure of seeing him in a clerical funk, I could almost be an onlooker. But the boys I hear are up, and it's time to be off."

" I'm saying, Melethor"— the burly Markus spoke what he had now to say with some hesitation—" I once mentioned the thing to you before, but you mustn't take it amiss—it positively is a fact : there's a growing report that half the estate is Weatherby's."

" The old story about my father's wishing to leave him Bletherentlet and Hurlit Valley. Is that clash not laid yet? I asked Rollockson, who tells me there never was any such intention. A propagation, man, of the parasites, who would fain have the eating of him up—that, and partly

Weatherby's own cockle-brained conceit.
I suppose they think it a fine joke to fill
the silly fellow's head; nay, I'm told they
have got the facetious length of calling
him Bletherentlet. When are you to be
out ?"

" Soon: to-morrow or next day. I have
to run over to see Kipperness about his
new steading; after that I am yours. I
suppose I may bring the pipes and everything as formerly for this turn yet ?"

The young men, laughing after their
grave, far-seeing Norse fashion, turned
their faces seaward from the brow of the
little cape to which they had ascended.
Beneath, on their left, lay Oyster Sound,
pale and still, with the *Tom Tub* and
Captain Kith and his people at breakfast;
on their right the open sea, the cool air of
which felt potent and refreshing after the

night's carouse. But scarce have the loving eyes saluted the expanse ere Markus Skeldar—unbonneted the gigantic hero stands, enjoying his brow-bath—suddenly utters a loud exclamation :

" Hallo ! what's yon over Scapaway Head ? I say, Melethor, you had better let that blast out before you sail."

" Hush, Markus ! I see it. I mean to give our new friend a taste of it; he was complaining last night of the calm. The fact is," said the Master, " I want to see what stuff he is made of. If he takes his ducking and his fright like a man, why there may be some hope of him yet."

Markus objected that the proposed test was irrelevant, inasmuch as a ducking was what no black-coat of any denomination could stand. Melethor begged his pardon ;

he knew more than one good fellow belonging to the cloth who could. Caldwel Gilchrist himself could; and *his* sense of comfort, and what was due to him from the clerk of the weather, was not far short of a prelate's.

They descended to the house. He summoned his brethren, and shaking hands with their friend they again embarked and set sail, the young men being still too much absorbed in their last night's cups to notice the threatening appearance of the weather outside. Markus Skeldar, whose huge Norse brain no amount of liquor could bedim, followed them round the shore, not exactly apprehensive, but certainly interested to see how they got through the approaching squall. With a clergyman on board—of a new and purer breed too—Markus calculated they would have a tussle for it with old Daddy Shordo —a boon name for the clerk.

What could Logan Morland ever hope to know of these men? How break down their social and class exclusivism, or work to any profit an old worn-out ground so strewn with the dust and bones of the primitive superstition?

CHAPTER VII.

LOGAN UNDERTAKING TO INSTRUCT HIS FELLOW-PASSENGERS
IN THE LAW OF STORMS, IS DISAGREEABLY INTERRUPTED.

THE Master saluted his passengers with a
brief " Good morning !" and the young men
nodded a more friendly " How are you ?"
Meanwhile, the sails were hoisted, and
they slid out of Oyster Sound before the
light matin breeze, Captain Kith in the
stern-sheets chattering to the poorer passengers, who seemed all as happy as possible in the prospect of soon being home.

They had a pleasant run in the cool glittering sunrise, during which my friend commented on the fine morning, and made such advances as he thought incumbent on him to the principal personage on board; but his overtures were coldly received. In about a quarter of an hour they had run through Blowerness. As they opened the northern main, with the tremendous cliffs of Scapaway and Redcraigs, sometimes called the Blawarts, confronting them, oh! then——

"Turn! turn back!" shouted Markus Skeldar from the shore. But they were too far out by the time he reached the point where he hoped to intercept them, and his powerful voice, exerted to the utmost, fell short in a hundred fathoms water.

Jerrold, surnamed by his brethren the Jollyboat, on account of his jovial con-

dition and argumentative propensity to
carry all along with him, was the first to
observe their danger.* " Gude be here,
lads," cried the young fellow, starting up ;
" do you see what a state Scapaway's in ?
and it's past to turn now, the tide will be
here in no time."

" In every stitch of canvas, and rig the
storm-jib ! Look alive, men. It's worse
than I thought," said the Master.

In an instant all was bustle, confusion,
and dismay. Our parson, however, did
not immediately catch the alarm. There
was nothing, it seemed to him, in the appearance quoted to justify so much appre-
hension ; he saw at a distance of a mile
or two a range of high cliffs, and a huge

---

* I put in a note here to say that Jerrold, poor fellow,
with all his exuberance—the Jollyboat as we used to call him
—is now where there are neither stories nor story-tellers ; he
died young.

lump of a hill, with a quantity of blackish vapour streaming at its summit—all the rest of the sky being perfectly clear; and Logan in his heart set them down—Master and men—as gasconading poltroons; an opinion which had been gaining upon him for several hours. There might be a bit of a breeze by-and-by off the cliffs, which were of a dark-red colour, and certainly looked grim and lowering : they were fast approaching them; and as this appeared to be a good opportunity of instructing his ignorant islanders in the laws and phenomena of storms, he said, still addressing himself to the Master, "Do you think the danger so imminent, sir ? I see none : the sky is quite healthy : these spiral-looking fogs at the top of that hill are purely local, the evaporation of last night's rain."

" Look here," said the Master; " do you
see that white rent on the water out
yonder ?"

" I see something white — a sort of
ripple——"

" It will be here immediately. That
ripple goes by the name of the tide with
us, and the last night's rain (you are
perfectly correct there, sir) has drawn
up on Redcraigs to give it battle. You
are in luck, Mr. Morland. In a couple
of minutes' time you will get the finest
dandling you have had since you were in
the nurse's arms !"

But to the last our parson sturdily abode
by his own opinion.

Effie, more observant if less learned
than her brother, formed a correcter estimate of their position. In the anxious
faces of all on board she saw that no light
thing was going to happen. Just as the

storm was about to burst on them, the Master asked her if she would like to see it, or whether she had not better lie down with the rest of the women : his manner, in the excitement of the crisis, was stern, though he did not mean it, and Effie took the hint and crept out of the way as well as she could.

It was just at hand. "Will you steer, Kith ? or shall I ?" said the Master.

"You had better let me," said Jerrold the Jollyboat, springing from his perch on the half-deck.

His brother put him down. Captain Kith, looking very pale but firm, replied, "I never flinched yet. I'll steer if you think I should, Mr. Melethor, but I would sooner trust the helm to yourself than any of us; not but what Mr. Jerrold's a very good hand at the helm too, but this"— the captain paused, and in a low voice added—" this will need a', baith land and lair, to bring us through."

Logan describes the meeting between wind and tide as beyond description terrific. He got a glimpse of the latter charging at full gallop a little way astern, and Redcraigs and Scapaway up in front blackening all that quarter of the heavens, and for a time he was in a kind of ecstasy or trance, whether of terror or of heroism he could never afterwards determine; but this he always maintained, that his senses never for an instant forsook him.

In these hurricanes everything depends on the man at the helm—a false turn of the rudder may consign all to the bottom; and for half an hour, while the gale was at worst, not a word was spoken. The men stood at their posts, watching the trim of the boat; the poor people, chiefly women, were stowed away under the half-deck, and occasionally a haggard face might be seen looking out, and as quickly withdrawn, as again and again the vessel, in the agony of convulsion, rose foaming at the prow. There was one very old woman who sometimes muttered audibly, "Oh, sirs! oh, sirs! God pity her—all her pretty young men!" And Captain Kith and the Master in the stern-sheets kept an eye to every wave. Terrible eyes they were to Effie, who saw them all the while. Twice she thought they were down; indeed, my friend assures me it was touch-and-go with them.

At length, however, the more imminent peril was past, and the boat, extricated from the crash of the tide (Captain Kith called it jabble), had now only the wind to contend with. Still it required some courage to look these tremendous cliffs in the face—they were now very near—as under storm-jib and mainsail they bore past them, rising sheer and shoreless, all shattered and blood-red to the height of several hundred feet, while the sun, just dipping from under the receding blast, threw over them a fitful illumination that gave to their aspect a still more portentous glare.

At this crisis the brandy-bottle did the state some service. Jerrold the Jollyboat candidly confessed he had not got such a fright since he was baptised, and regretted it had not occurred to him sooner to take a little Dutch courage. "Here's to us, lads!" He strongly recommended his tall and handsome brother Weatherby, by the title of Lord London, to confess and take a little drop too; but lack of courage in any shape was a thing Mr. Weatherby would never hear of—having but too good cause, some of his friends thought. He had, however, no objections to the brandy; so he tossed off his glass, and retorting the imputation cast upon his courage, was very witty on the Jollyboat's white nose, appealing to all round whether they had not seen it go white. Captain Kith, a judicious person in such squabbles, could not say that he had.

" White !" cried the Jollyboat himself, " of course it did; such a screed as that away past was enough to take the dye out of old Dropogrog's nose, let alone the natural colour of a young beginner's !"

The cup was proffered to Morland in his turn; and our friend had the good sense to profit so much by his dram as to enjoy the remainder of the voyage—with here and there an exceptional twinge, perhaps, when the boat, under the afflatus that bore her along, was laid a little—a very little—too near the gunwale's edge.

There is unquestionably an excitement in tearing along in three hundred fathoms water past these enormous red cliffs that front to the North Sea; but for myself I must frankly own with friend Logan I would dispense with again experiencing the grand emotion. Such tempests are frequent in the Orkney Islands; they generally cease as suddenly as they arise, in some instances embracing a circuit of only a very few miles, and lasting no longer than till the foul fog that engendered them is spent. The sun was again shining out, and, all talk and animation, they bore up for Hallow. Captain Kith having let out the women, sat chattering to them like an ape; and even the envoy forgot that he was a stranger.

Not so Effie. She sat up with the rest, but the joy of escape was dashed by the humiliating conviction that they were unwelcome intruders. This appeared not only in the guarded aversion of the Master, but at times still more cuttingly in the careless observations of the younger lads. And so this was Hallow—dear Hallow, as Mr. Bland would have it that evening he came out expressly and drank tea with them at Chapel-end (unrecorded)—the paradise which that tender and imaginative divine had extolled to the skies, where the people were *so* simple, *so* kind, *so* affectionate? Had he wilfully deceived them, or was the man merely rhapsodising at his ease from the force of habit? This was a wicked thought, but it was perfectly natural, and Effie could not help it. The heart will use strong, nay, coarse, expressions at times, and never trouble the tongue to utter them: in her heart Effie called Bland a humbug! The novelty of the scene, however (for now she under-

stood they were approaching their destination), soon chased away those evil ima-
ginations.

They landed at the village of Sandyhaven,
the capital of Hallow Isle. Mrs. Deerness,
accompanied by half the population of the
place, was waiting to receive them. Her
countenance expressed feelings of gratitude
too deep for utterance. She stood on the
pier until the boat touched shallow water
—it broke out then : " Oh, boys, I am so
thankful to have you all safe back !" and
she kissed them one after another as they
jumped on shore.

" By my sowl, and so you may, mamma!"
cried the Jollyboat.

Effie, an anxious onlooker — for what
else but the women of the family had she
to put hope in ?—Effie, I say, was pleased
with her reply to the bluff caress. " Down,
and don't tear my gown, you great, big——"

she said, affectionately pushing the exuberant cub away to make room for others— Captain Kith and crew, and the humbler sharers of their escape. It is difficult to find an exact term for the kind of fascination which seemed to be the special endowment of this extraordinary woman, but what is meant will appear more clearly as we go on.

Her family and numerous dependents disposed of, the Lady of Hallow received the envoy of the Church with the courtesy to which his credentials entitled him, but with none of the empressement which at that time characterised the greetings between the evangelical pastor and the wealthier subjects of his flock. She asked more questions, indeed, respecting the movement than Logan could fully answer; but they sounded to him as put rather in a spirit of carping inquiry than of zealous

attachment to the cause. In this, however, his ear exaggerated a little; he was
jaded after his long journey, and, besides,
he overlooked the fact that, in a remote
situation, there is no more natural feeling
than this sort of curiosity respecting trivial
details.

In the mean time, Effie surveyed the
adopted isle. Hallow is rather a pretty
island. It rises gradually towards the
middle, and is crowned by a natural tumulus, somewhat resembling in shape one
of those artificial earthen mounds, the
justice hills of ancient litigation. The
harvest was begun in scattered patches,
and extending as far back as the bare stony
girdle round the tumulus on the summit,
had a most pleasing effect to the eye,
which was enhanced by the little home-
steads shining in the sun.

She was still more pleased with Hallow

House. Effie feared to see some grand
piece of modern architecture, offensive to
her brother's Whiggish pride, and was glad
to find an antique jumble upwards of two
hundred years old, bearing date 1607. The
house is backed by mighty barns, generally
open to the breeze of summer, but round
which the excluded winter winds whistle
and rave, or gurgle in rainy weather with
yet more impressive sough. The kitchen-
chimney, a huge tunnel of red and grey
stone, towers over all the others. A low,
circular-arched gateway at the end of the
little street admits into the feudal domain;
passing from the haven through this por-
tal, it is about as far again to the front
door of the house. The grass is close
cropped and beautifully green, and not far
from the door stands a doddered old thorn,
the only tree in the island. After a while
the absence of trees is less felt in this mass

of solitary green all around, as drawing up beside the rugged hospitable mansion you face the broad Atlantic, and look out on its expanse, with the village of Sandyhaven lying at your feet.

CHAPTER VIII.

HALLOW HOUSE: A DESCRIPTION OF THE FAMILY AND
FIRESIDE.

LOGAN would have preferred stepping at once into his own parsonage had that been possible; but as matters stood, he was constrained to accept the lady's invitation to be their inmate for a day or two.

Old Mr. Deerness, too ill to sit at table, but still taking his single glass of wine by the fireside, did much to reconcile my friend to his temporary residence in the great house.

The hospitable dying old man asked him
such flattering questions as occurred to
him concerning the new Church. Effie
was much affected by his goodness, over-
clouded as he appeared to be by some secret
sorrow; it was painful to her at times to
see the wandering, and, as it were, lost expression of his face. Like his sons, he had
been handsome in his youth.

The conversation at table was cheerful,
though subdued, in respect to the old gentleman at the fireside; it became even ani-
mated when Mr. Deerness, his hospitable
spirits rising, drank a second glass of wine
in honour of the envoy, saying he felt so
much better to-day. As he made the remark, mother and sons exchanged a look
of sad affection. He did not appear to Morland to distinguish one above another—
Mr. Weatherby, who was his namesake,
more than his brethren. He had an old-

fashioned custom of drinking to their healths separately as he sipped his wine.

Respecting the grand question, Logan saw that his new friends had much to learn. This was to be expected of the lads. But, in the conversation of Mrs. Deerness herself, he was surprised to find an amount of ignorance wholly inconsistent with her repute at head-quarters, and absolutely at variance with Bland's refined gold. Ignorance, too, of a complicated and peculiar kind, some of her mistakes obviously arising from the newspapers, those deluders, as he would have it, of the public mind, though that did not account for all. Often she was misinformed, wrong in her facts, or, if right in her facts, wrong in her deductions; sometimes wrong altogether; denying the law of patronage in one sentence, asserting it obliquely in the next; now blaming government, now the Church;

full of this man's speech, doubting and re-
jecting that other's, and the latter, perhaps,
the greater gun of the two. And so of the
leading articles: some of Messieurs the
Editors caught it! but Logan had no objection to that. Now conforming to the
principles of the Retreat as they were beginning to be practically acted upon; anon
facing about on the Residuaries, she proposed to return and rout the whole car-
nality, to drive out the old wretches since
they would not come out. In short, to
make root and branch work whilst they
were about it, annihilate the * * * * * *
(naming a leading influential journal),
excommunicate the government, and burn
the lords ordinary, those wicked wizards
on the corrupt side of the Church!

Upon the whole, all this rather astonished
our friend. After the circulation of a moderate glass, the boys would have him out

to see the island; and in the interim, Effie was shown all over the house by Mrs. Deerness. A fine, rambling collection it was, abounding in little old bedrooms on different levels, long passages and galleries, and no fewer than three staircases—just the sort of house for children to scamper up and down in of a rainy day, and for young people come to more reflective years to traverse at eve, and enjoy the setting in of the autumn chill. In this manner was Effie following her hostess from room to room, taking the saddened but really exquisite pleasure one feels in a scene entirely new, when she was startled, and, truth to say, very much frightened, by an unexpected ebullition of feeling. Nothing hitherto could exceed the kindness of Mrs. Deerness, or the simple, grand urbanity of her manner. What might have been the immediate cause Effie could not conceive; but all at once, the Imp of Mischief, who goes about in the twilight, jingled at the lady's ear that same mystical bunch of missing keys.

Some of the effects of this aggressive form of the religious melancholy are so fully brought out by Markus Skeldar in his table conversation, that I again take leave to quote that benighted worthy:

" I'll tell you what it is, sir," Markus, tabling his huge fist, would say, "they may call it by this kirk or that kirk, but the thing in a very short time will be a personal feud with her with every man, woman, and child she comes across. A year or two ago, before this sect appeared, a more splendid woman never sat at the head of a table. But now! To hear her now! I defy you to sit and hear her on these old beggars of Residuaries, as they call them, without feeling that all the time you are getting your Residuary skelps yourself. One hates to be deboshed in that way. Hang it, can't she speak plain out to a fellow's face!"

Effie, a nicer judge than Mr. Skeldar, thought that the attack was of the nature of fits—the hysterica passio of Lear—a morbid and somewhat overstrained sense of man's ingratitude, similar to that which made the old king break out upon his thankless daughters. The first of which she was a witness was thus described by Effie to her brother:

"We were a little tired after wandering all over the house, and were standing at one of the windows, looking out on the sea, when I noticed that her attention seemed suddenly startled by something, and then the fit seized her. Thinking that I must have somehow given offence, I cannot tell you what I felt. It is really impossible to repeat all she said—the numbers she sent to the ill place. I never heard anything in or out of the pulpit like it. The fit lasted five or six minutes, perhaps, and left her just as suddenly as it came on."

" Describe her appearance at the termination of the fit, as you call it," said the parson.

" She just stopped speaking," said Effie. " When I looked up, her eye was fixed calmly on the setting sun ; there was but a small bit of the red disc above water ; and I saw that the fit was over. She said to me with a smile, like a person exhausted, ' But what nonsense all this must be to you, Miss M., after your long journey.' After that," added Effie, " I could not describe her kindness—asking all about us, about our father and mother—and how long it was since we lost them. God help her, Logan ! She may be capricious and changeable, and may be at times more outspoken than you could wish, but I canna help thinking it's all along of that dying auld man in the chimney corner."

"Possibly, Effie. I think in that idea you may not be far wrong," replied the parson.

But this was not all : already there were things which prudence forbade Effie to speak of even to her brother. Effie had not seen much of the world, but she had seen enough to know that a mark of con-fidence is not always necessarily a mark of favour. A mark, then, of confidence, con-sidering that she was an entire stranger to Mrs. Deerness, surprised Effie very much, and was further illustrative of the impulsive character of the Lady of Hallow.

She spoke as freely of her own private affairs as she had been frank and cordial in her inquiries about her young guest's by-past days; of Mr. Deerness being in dying circumstances; that he was a good man, but being naturally so, she was at times oppressed with the uncertainty of whether he was in a state of grace, and that often, very often, she had it in her heart to speak to him on the subject, but as yet she had never been able to find words to do it. This to a stranger was going pretty far, but the Lady of Hallow went further.

" You would observe, Miss Morland, the remarkable likeness of my second son to his father." (Miss Morland intimated that she had.) "And perhaps you also noticed that Mr. Deerness has at times a more overcast and thinking look than you would ascribe to a person in his condition, as if he were brooding over some past sorrow ?" (Effie said she thought it might be bodily pain.) "No, my dear! Mr. Deerness has but little bodily pain, but he has a sorrow that will never quit him till he leaves this world—a sorrow, to use the language of this world, God knows lightly incurred—a sorrow unknown to my oldest son—known only to himself and me. It originated many years ago. It was at a friend's house : they were dining, and Mr. Deerness took a little too much; as for the others, they were every one more intoxicated than another. My husband made no distinction between any of the boys ; but he had a work with his namesake—the little fellow was so like him— poor Raby ! A quarrel arose among them at table—a lairds' quarrel about the land —when Mr. Trigilgas of Kipperness, who had a sneering, provoking tongue, said something that irritated Mr. Deerness, and in the passion of the moment he vowed a solemn vow that he would split Hallow, and leave his second son a better laird

than would ever stand in the shoes of the
Cock of Kipperness—for so in sport the
oldest, and indeed the only, son of Kipperness was named. It was but an incon-
siderate vaunt, made at a drunken meeting, and yet it has been an unceasing
sorrow to Mr. Deerness. He mentioned
the circumstance to me when he came
home, saying he regretted it very much;
however, we both agreed that it would be
forgotten. But it was not forgotten—such
things are not forgotten—and Mr. Deerness eventually gave up going into society.
It will now be six or seven years ago that
he told me he intended going no more out.
Old Kipperness was dead, and young Kip
in his place, though he would be forty
when he succeeded to the property: 'The
Cock of Kipperness could crow now; when
might they expect the Cock of Bletherentlet to crow back to him?' Mr. Deerness

was not a man to put up with their vulgar
gibes. But society was the spring of his
life. None of his sons, Miss Morland, can
give you an adequate idea of him. Melethor is much cleverer—at least his talents
have been more cultivated—but he has not
the hearty simplicity of his father; and,
from the day he took to the fireside, I
observed the declining change upon Mr.
Deerness," &c., &c.

Your country lady, like your country
laird, has no doubt the privilege of being
a discursive talker, but Effie was certainly
surprised that such a communication
should have been made to her. Why was
it made ? From the pure love of serious
gossip ? In some of the more natural
strokes it seemed so, but still there seemed
something behind—it had the air of a half-
communication, and half-communications
are always suspicious. For instance, the

frequent reference to her second son, the handsome Weatherby, was generally in such terms that Effie, for the life of her, could not make out whether Weatherby was a favourite with his mother or not. At first sight the family likeness was strong in all, yet there was great diversity of character.

The following table will perhaps be of some help here:

1. Melethor, commonly called the Master. The young laird.

2. Weatherby, familiarly Mr. Raby. Profession not known. Nicknames, Lord London and Lugs' Heir.

3. William, surnamed the Institute. The Scotch Bar.

4. Jerrold, surnamed the Jollyboat. Commerce. An extensive merchant.

5. Harriet, Miss Deerness.

6. Eric, surnamed the Grouse. The

Navy. Grouse was but a little chap of fifteen, short and squat, but a very comical, lovable little fellow, who promised to be every inch a sailor.

Miss Deerness was from home on a visit; of her, more in another place.

The next three in succession, upwards, were tall, handsome youths, rejoicing in locks of jet, and that kind of figure which promises to become a little ducal in after years. Jerrold was already corpulent. His florid, handsome, open countenance renders any comment on his particular character unnecessary.

William, who was destined to be a lawyer, was the quietest of the lot, but possessed talents more nearly up to the mark than any of the others, Melethor alone excepted. He had a good deal of quiet humour, a keen sense of the ludicrous, and, lawyer-like, had already the knack of setting his two right and left hand brethren at comic loggerheads.

Weatherby, in stature, approached the colossal; his complexion was the perfection of pale, and so far as symmetry of features constitutes beauty, the fellow was undoubtedly very handsome. In character he was more complex than a ravelled skein of thread. He was a coxcomb, and yet not a coxcomb—he could forget that he was handsome for days together. He had popular manners—when he chose—but even in that matter he was unequal. He affected cleverness, and sometimes said a smart thing enough. Some people thought him really clever—others an ass. In short, people differed in their opinions of him, as much as the three travellers about the chameleon, and probably from a similar cause—the young man's external susceptibility of change: properly, Wea-

therby had no character at all but the nature or the knack of reflecting in a great
measure the kind of opinion that was
brought to bear upon him. He was a
great puzzle to our parson, as we shall
by-and-by have occasion to see.

Melethor, again, was a different being
altogether in appearance, as in temper,
talents, and education. He was not so
tall as his three brethren, though above
the middle height — a spare, handsome,
smart figure of a man, straight-backed,
and well made: the raven locks of the
mother had in his case a tawny wave, and
the Norse blue predominated in his eye,
and the shrewd hardy face had a beauty
of its own, though not of the voluptuous
cast. In Melethor the personal attraction
was originality; he did not care a farthing
to know whether or not he was thought
handsome, but he would have fought the

devil, had the father of lies said he did not look like a gentleman.

And here, while we are on the subject of these Hallow youths, it may be proper to notice a little difference of opinion between Effie and her brother. The third or fourth evening, as they were taking a walk by themselves, Logan, who probably through Bland had got hold of the popular notion respecting the division of the property, and the restoration of the second branch, expressed higher opinions of Mr. Weatherby than, as will be found, he was afterwards disposed to maintain.

"To-day," he said, "he and I had a long walk together. How little should we judge by externals! With a good deal of the fop in his manners, and certainly very much in his appearance, I found him really an agreeable young man, of amiable sentiments and remarkably orthodox

views. A great comfort to the mother,
poor lady! for if I am not very much mistaken, I plainly foresee that the others will
not be long with her; it seems pretty clear
to me that that old leaven kinsman Caldwel Gilchrist they speak of has the making
up of their minds as certainly as a baker
the baking of his penny baps. I was as
much struck as pleased with the young
man's concern about his soul."

" Don't talk such horrid nonsense, Logan," said Effie, in a low, scared voice;
"I'm not saying the young man's a hypo-
crite—I dare say he may be in a fright
about his soul—but what I mean is, for
mercy's sake do not encourage Mrs. Deerness to place her happiness in *him* particularly. Did ever you hear such a laugh
as he has? He reminds me of the whale
we saw on the passage from the steamer's
deck, seldom coming to the surface but

when he has to blow. So unlike the rest
of his brothers in all his ways, depend upon
it, though he were to pray seven times in
the day, he's not to be trusted."

Logan replied more angrily than I care
to set down against poor dear Effie; and
yet before many days his opinions of Mr.
Weatherby Deerness were pretty nearly
identical with hers.

CHAPTER IX.

THE PARSON AT HOME—PREPARATIONS FOR HIS FIRST SERMON
—INTERVIEW OF THE MASTER WITH HIS KINSMAN, THE
PRIEST OF STIFRAKNESS.

THE third succeeding day saw the Morlands settled in their own humble abode,
a paradise to Effie had it been in any
sense their own; but the furniture—everything, the very chair she sat on crying—
had all come from the great house. Foolish
tears, Logan said — ungrateful, selfish,
sinful. What absurd—he might almost
call it insane—kind of carnal importance

was it she attached to the necessity of things being their own? Considerations of this kind certainly did not disturb our friend—that is to say, when mounted on his hobby; afoot, he was a sturdy, independent fellow enough.

The cottage was new, having been built for the bailiff, or land steward, whom it was thus put·past, not a little, by the way, to that gentleman's disgust. It was commodious for its size—Mr. Bailiff had seen to that—and very prettily situated on the margin of a winding fresh-water lake, with one or two other cottages in sight. The "braes" were covered with rabbits, and nothing could be prettier than to see them in the early morning capering about or sitting washing their faces. There was a mill-wheel within hearing, evidently, from its deliberate and subdued click-clack, fed by no very lavish stream; the plash of it could be seen just round the point op-posite to the manse door.

However, if the furniture was not *de facto* their own, the parson's upholstering genius, by arranging and rearranging, speedily gave things a more feasible aspect, even in Effie's eyes. The greatest difficulty she had was with their maid-servant Char-lotte Kith, a daughter of the captain's.

Tsharlotte, as the captain pronounced the name, had been entered at Halloy House; but as her first twelvemonths' term did not expire till Martinmas, the girl had not seen much ; indeed, it was doubt-ful whether another term would have much improved her—she was something deficient in personal comeliness to take heartily to service. In short, it was plain to Effie that her colleague Charlotte was no witch. From her manner of going about things, it was really difficult to de-

termine whether she was asleep or awake;
the thing seemed a dream to her; and on
some points, such as singing or laughing
at improper times, the difference between
mistress and maid, her understanding
appeared to be hopelessly clouded; the
ignorant neophyte, dazzled by the light of
the new doctrines, went singing and
dreaming about the house, as if she were
in love with her mistress, or mistook her
for a veritable angel. And thus, in place
of a servant, Effie had a partisan. Then
again, the girl's untutored questions respecting the new dynasty were sometimes
difficult enough to answer — as, for example, "Was it the millennium in the ald
prophets, the lang thousand years'?"

Nor when the parson came home in the
evening (after his first day's pastoral
round), did the presence of her master,
imposing as that ought to have been,

work the miracles Effie expected, as the following instance will amply suffice to prove. Brother and sister were sat down for the evening ; Effie was writing to her friend Mary Fletcher, and Logan was deep in the composition of his first sermon, when suddenly the silence of the parlour was broken by a strange, wheezing, uncouth laugh of exultation at his back, that reminded him of friend Leatherbreeches in Princes-street, and caused him to feel for the moment as if he had been caught up by the hair of the head : it was Kith, overlooking the progress of the good work ! " I wish Sabbath was the morn !" said the odd girl, and retreated as stealthily as she had come in.*

Next day, in the course of his goings out and in, Logan took occasion to state his

---

* An instance of the attachment of the peasantry to their ancient mode of observing the Sabbath.—ED.

mind more definitively on the subject. "Effie," said he, "you will have to get rid of that girl, she's mad. I tell you she's perfectly deranged."

"Not she," said Effie; "she's only a little odd."

"Well, as you will," rejoined Logan; "the girl is more in your department than mine. But recollect I told you. And at all events," he added, "if you must or will keep her, tell her she is not to grin and laugh in my face every time she meets me."

"She can't help it," said Effie.

"How! what!" cried the parson.

"I mean," explained Effie, "that it's an hysterical affection, and she can't help it. She's the same to me."

"Umph!" And the subject was dropped for the present.

The prevalence of this seemingly dubious kind of sanity among his parishioners was a great grief to the young parson. At length he learned that there was a crazy fanatic of a hedge-preacher in the island, of the name of Ingles, who ought to be put down, as a fosterer of this dwarfed and distorted sort of intellect; but the fellow, he informed Effie, was as cunning as a fox, and he had not yet obtained a sight of him. "He goes," added Logan, "by the name of Rob of the Bog." 	.

Another on his list of Rob's proselytes was Weatherby Deerness. "I don't understand that young fellow at all," said the parson. "There unquestionably is a want about him : forward in his manner, and yet not frank; given to ramble, yet a listless idler at home; a fop in his dress, yet moody as the melancholy Jacques; a loud laugher, louder than his brethren, but it does not ring out: how different from the prolonged bellow of Jerrold, whom they call the Jollyboat! To-day, I questioned the three younger lads why they called him Lugs' Heir, when Jerrold, *more suo*, replied, 'By my feth, parson, you had best not call him that to his face!' William, a quiet, sensible lad, told me aside that Lugs was the name given to an old family ghost, and—and, in short, they did not like to hear it spoken of."

Meanwhile, Mrs. Deerness was not idle. A barn, suitable for the purpose, having been selected, the wrights were busy fitting it up as a temporary church. Care was taken never to omit the word *temporary*, thus clearly implying the intention of building a more permanent edifice. During these preparatory movements, there was one topic of frequent recurrence in the speculations of the lady and the envoy— how, namely, would their neighbour across the water be feeling ? what saying to their doings ? or would the matter have yet reached the ears of the old gentleman ? Very likely not.

The ancient Residuary, however, was not quite so dormant as they fancied. He was surveying the ground and taking counsel with himself. In the mean time, a reverend brother, in a mainland parish, undertook to sound the Master.

This gentleman, the Reverend Caldwel Gilchrist, was nearly related to the Hallow family. He was a churchman of the Church, a gentlemanly man of the world that is to say; of moderate abilities, prim manners, a cold temper, and, as a matter of course, an ignorer of dissent in all its forms. Hearing that his kinsman was to be over in the neighbourhood shooting, he invited him to dinner: they dined, and had some conversation afterwards, when

Mr. Gilchrist was considerably disappointed to find the young laird less decidedly on their side than he had hoped.

"I should not," he said, "expect your father, considering the state of his health, to be at the trouble to interfere. But I must own, my dear Melethor, I am surprised—I may say more than surprised—at *your* submission——"

"Why, look you here," said the Master, "I am neither theologian nor Church politician, and what, perhaps, concerns the matter more, I am not laird. You alluded to my father. I may tell you flatly and frankly, Mr. Gilchrist, I won't have my father's last days embittered by your Church squabbles."

"There might be a worse preparation for his change," observed Mr. Gilchrist, a little tartly, "than his taking part with the Church of his forefathers, deserted and maligned as it is by a set of half-mad, half-hypocritical visionaries. But, waving that," he added, more temperately, and changing the ground, "I don't see the application of your objection. Why should *your* interference cause any annoyance to your father? He need never hear of it."

"You forget my mother," was the Master's significant reply.

"It is true, then, that she is as strong on that side as report says?" .

Melethor gave no direct answer to this question. "You may thank yourselves for all this," he said.

"Drink your wine, my dear Melethor," said his reverend cousin. "You are in an ill humour."

"I am not in a very good one," said Melethor. "I repeat it—you have yourselves to thank. I don't refer to your Church corruption—whether it was so great as they say, and all that : I dare say there was a good deal of vulgar exaggeration; but, had the thing been taken in time, with a little common sense, and a little common exertion, this explosion might have been avoided."

" Well," said the other ; " we need not discuss so wide and general a question as that.   But, in common courtesy to your minister, I think you ought to take up more decided ground."

" Do you call that vulgar old wretch my minister ?" answered the Master. " If Calthrop can't be at the trouble to look after his own affairs, he'll find himself in a mistake if he fancies it's because I am looking after them for him. The wonder in his case is that we have not had an interloper long ago. Did not Bland, that time he was down on his exploring mission, this time two years, tell my mother that he had nowhere in the whole course of his tour met with anything like it ? that there was no ignorance like the ignorance of Hallow ? And was not the sufficient reason this, that Calthrop was not over once in six weeks to preach to them ?"

" That fellow Bland," observed Mr. Gilchrist, " is a peevish, punctilious puritan. Did he expect to find poor people in Orkney as glib at reply to his whining questions as their town flocks in the south ? They are no worse in Hallow than their neighbours. And, if I recollect aright, your mother gave Mr. Bland but small thanks for his information."

The Master laughed, and said, jocularly, " Ay, marry was there something of that kind ! I forget now the exact terms she used, but I recollect that the Edinburgh divine had to cough and give in. I never saw a man make a cleaner pair of heels out of an argument."

" I can conceive it—served him right," said Caldwel. " But I am the more surprised she should take on with these people now, or attach so much weight to their representations."

" I am not at all surprised," said his blunt kinsman. " Why, look you, sir, it *is* the fact that the ignorance in Hallow is deplorable, and it is the fact that Calthrop seldom looks near them. Half a dozen sermons a year is rather short allowance."

" Then, what on earth," exclaimed the priest of Stifbakness, fairly losing his temper, " could make Markus Skeldar give me such an account of your sentiments as he did this morning ? The subject is out of his way, perhaps, but he must be a greater monster of stupidity than ever I took him for; he told me that you were decidedly opposed to these people— 'bitter' was the word."

"Bitter—but not at them in particular. My friend Markus, as you observe, is no great theological carrier. The fact is, I hate religious discord, and I foresee that we are to have a fine time of it."

"Surely," said Mr. Gilchrist, "I know nothing so vulgar, so deplorable. But should not that be a prime motive for keeping these people at a distance?"

"No, Mr. Gilchrist," said the other; "had Calthrop done his duty I might have had some pretext, but as it is, I have none. If you will have the truth, I am ashamed of the island. Things must take their course."

Very unsavoury conclusion this—anti-parochial, as Mr. Bumble has it." Says the dignified but distressed Caldwel, "I will speak to the Presbytery, to Calthrop himself; I will undertake that in future he does duty more regularly."

" As you please," replied his kinsman.

" How, sir ! am I to understand that if there is service in the parish church you will not attend ?"

" I may or I may not. I won't pledge myself."

" Or, if need be, compel your people to go ?" said Caldwel Gilchrist, in rising indignation.

" Most certainly not," replied the Master.

" Very well, my dear Melethor—*very* well, please yourself. I'm sorry for you. You will by-and-by have a fine hotbed of fanaticism upon your hands. And what is more, sir——"

" I am aware of all that, my dear Caldwel, but I must be going."

" Won't you stay and take a cup of tea and a hand? Eliza expects you."

" Well, I cannot.   I have to see Cults, and must be in Kirkwal to-night; so shake hands."

And so ended his visit to the priest of Stifbakness.

CHAPTER X.

LOGAN RENEWS HIS ACQUAINTANCE WITH MR. RALPH RUDDOCK
—HE MEETS IN THE ISLAND OF VENTUREFAIR MR. DAIDLE'S
TOWNSWOMAN, THE LONG-LOST SALLY BARON.

On the Saturday before Commencement Sunday Effie met Miss Deerness for the first time.

Harriet was a blooming girl of sixteen, frank, open, and conversable. Fresh from a boarding-school, there was nothing missyish about her; there was an earnest womanliness in her manner for one so young; no affectation, no attempt to say clever things, plain, cheerful talk and plenty of it; everything, in short, to be desired in a companion. Had Effie been at all read in the great bard (prohibited by Logan), she would at once have recognised in her new friend the Miranda of the isle.

But when they came to talk of the great theme, Effie could not avoid perceiving that Miss Deerness was a little deficient. Her notion of the difference between the old state of things and the new appeared to be all summed up in the laughing reply she made to a question from Effie respecting the venerable incumbent across the water. Effie, picturing to herself a venerable, though mistaken, old man, was anxious to compute the time when these unhappy differences should cease and her brother enjoy that clerical companionship without which his lot was, in the mean while, imperfect; so she asked what sort of person he was, and this was Miranda's description of him:

"You never saw such an ugly old man. He's always joking and showing his yellow teeth. And he eats sweeties while he's preaching, and that sets the boys a laughing in church when they see the stragglers falling over on old Jemmy Foster, the precentor, and Jemmy pretending to duck down his head, but all the while wetting his finger and picking them up as fast as he can."

Effie laughed at the anecdote. "But how," she asked, jokingly, "are the sweeties first got into the ministerial mill?"

"Oh, very simply. He makes up his cambric pocket-handkerchief in his hand—so—and when he has occasion to cough, the sweeties are there."

It was a burning, brilliant harvest day,

and in a saunter round the lake, that Effie thus made the acquaintance of Miss Deerness. In the mean time we are called by the parson's more important discoveries in the neighbouring island of Venture-fair.

Having employed Captain Kith to row him over, they were leisurely approaching that gem of the Orkneys. One half of the island consists of burnt rock without any shore—in the language of the country, a mool; but round the mool the other side is fair and fertile. They were in a small punt, only himself and the captain, and as the day was very fine and the parson in a beneficent humour, Captain Kith found him exceedingly chatty and agreeable. How deeply, too, was the captain impressed as he paddled along in front of the fire-blasted isle, with the pale, gleaming-eyed ecclesiastic intently inspecting every fissure and pore of the burnt rock! But when Logan, with uplifted forefinger desiring him to rest on his oars, gave him its whole geological history from beginning to end, the captain fairly thought himself bewitched. During the recital his colour went and came as if at every undulation of the deep still water he fancied it was another eruption beginning to boil up from below—as I make no doubt the captain did—for Logan possessed that minute and, as it were, professional faculty of describing the action of fire which, without his intending it, held his auditor's attention until the gallant captain literally grinned with agony. Most heartily glad, therefore, was Captain Kith when, quitting the terrors of the mool, they landed on the fertile side of the island in a beautiful bay, containing two or three houses.

"Is there anything to be had—can we

get any refreshment here?" inquired the parson.

" There was used," said the captain, " to be a public-hoos, but that was a long time ago, when it was a station" (for herring curing). " However, I'll not say but fat it may be there yet. They was used to keep ale—peri weak stuff to be sure, and little sib to fat it suld be—but malt's aye thicker than water," quoth the captain, " and it'll not tak 's long to mak a ca'."   •

Readers will understand from this speech of Captain Kith's that they brewed famous strong ale at the Hall House in Hallow.

A short walk along the beach brought them to the public-house, which was still there. But the name on the signboard over the door had a repellant effect on Captain Kith, not less instantaneous than had the handwriting that appeared on the

wall to King Belshazzar : he drew back
with an aghast expression, while the parson, thinking it some piece of superstitious idolatry, asked him sharply what he
meant by exhibiting such slavish terror at
sight of a common signboard over a house
of public entertainment.

"It's the lost favourite—her as was called
Sally Baron," said the captain, speaking
very rapidly and in a low voice; "once in
a weel-to-do way about the hoos owerby,
and muckle thought o' she was—a braw
besom she was—she was childer-maid and
had charge o' the childer. But the leddy
and her quarrelled, and Madam Sally got
the pack—and pack she did—some said on
a broomstick; but I don't think so much
about that as the curse o' an angry woman,
and to all appearance of a starving woman,
forby, for her name was prohibit from that
day furth, and now here it's on a public-

hoos as white 's a leper, this twenty year
kenned for poverty without and poverty
within. Safe and keep us, minister, if I like
this ava! Turn your back, sir," added
the captain, hastily suiting the action to
the word in his own person; " I see the
face glowerin at 's through the dirty win-
nock !"

Logan, in fact, did perceive the outline
of a human countenance at one window on
the ground-floor of the tenement while he
was surveying the dilapidated exterior, and
wondering by what capricious turn of fortune it had attained to the wretchedness
of a second story: as for the other houses,
they appeared to have no inhabitants at
all, and the whole place had a look of evil
omen, the more depressing from its exhibiting the marks of former trade, such
as iron rings and mooring-posts, and there
was a kind of fishy smell.

It was to this the parson paid the natural tribute of a sigh, not to the captain's
legend, though it had old Daidle's story to
back it.

" You are superstitious, my dear captain," said he ; " the poor malice of a dis-
carded servant is not likely to have sur-
vived so long, even should this woman be
the same you refer to. Enter and ascer-
tain whether we can have any refreshment."

They entered accordingly. The landlady,
an odd-looking woman, very meanly clad,
but with some grey ringlets escaping from
under a coif that might have seen better
days, merely stared in answer to the chattering captain's civil " How's a' wi' us the
day, mistress ?" And the ale was as little
akin to that genial beverage as the captain
had predicted. With regard to the woman
herself, he was obliged to confess he could

not be absolutely certain whether she was the person or not. Now, nothing annoyed Logan more than this sort of wavering weakness. Captain Kith, however, replied appositely enough, " That, as far as the short look he got of her gaed, he thought she was the same, but ye maun mind, minister, its twenty year syne, and that and the bra claes maks a difference."

" Do they call this ale?" said the parson, indignantly. " I cannot perceive that it has the most distant resemblance to ale. Is there no other house—nothing better to be had than this wretched trash?"

The captain was afraid not. " Except your Reverence was to gie the laird a ca' and bid him draw 's bottle on 's."

" The laird?—the proprietor of the island, you mean : who is he?"

" Ou, deed, sir, no very muckle fan a' 's done," replied Captain Kith ; " deest that weary peri body, Balph Ruddock. There's other two proprietors forby, but they don't live in the island, and so Balph's like king o' the whole."

" Aha !" cried Logan, " I am then in the country of my friend Mr. Ruddock. And that I suppose is his house on the other side of the creek ?"

" That's his hoos round the voe; they call it the Hall," said the captain; " and so, since your Reverence kens Balph, he'll canna help himsel'—he must draw 's bottle on 's."

But, either disregarding or not observing that the captain spoke in the plural, Logan left him to finish the jug, while he himself posted round the little bay to call on his friend Mr. Ruddock, whose seat, situated near the mouth of a small rivulet, was snugly secluded from all winds save the south. There seemed to be a garden of some sort behind.

The parson, taking his stick to it, gave a good hearty, cheerful knock at the door. It was opened by a small elderly man in a dock-tail-coat and pantaloons—the crab-apples in his cheeks might denote indifferent health, and perhaps a spice of irascibility. No ordinary penetration could have divined for a moment that this was Balph's brother, Mr. Petrie. Logan, supposing him to be the butler, asked if his master was at home, and received for answer a loud " No !"

So loud, indeed, as to make our friend start: he begged pardon : "Is Mr. Ruddock at home ?"

" I believe I am all that's for him just at present," replied Mr. Petrie. " I believe I am at home, but can't just say for

certain—any letters? any peri testificate?
Name, if you please."

"Morland: the Reverend Logan Morland."

"Did you want anything, sir? We
stick to our own persuasion!" added Mr.
Petrie, hastily, the crab-apples in his
cheeks giving out a brighter flush of
nervous alarm.

"The poor man must be insane," thought
Logan, and was about to turn away, when
Mr. Petrie, ashamed of his stingy weak-
ness, threw wide the hospitable door.

"Step in, sir—step in; both glad to see
you."

So saying, he ushered the visitor into a
little dark parlour, he himself disappearing
in a closet off it, from which, after some
groping and jingling, he at length produced
the Hall bottle, and having poured out a
couple of glasses, Mr. Petrie proceeded

further to enact the hospitable landlord. He ran on:

"Your very good health, sir; we are happy to see you at Fair Hall. Your name, I think you said, was Kirkland."

" Morland, sir," corrected the envoy.

" *Mor*eland—very good—the modern style of it; Kirkland, the ancient, originally plain *Kirk*, afterwards changed to *more* by the figure habeas—you'll find the whisky very good. *One!*" (Mr. Petrie had a whimsical custom of counting his jokes, one, two, three, and so on, as they occurred.) "They tell a good story of one to the norrit of this, who, thinking to do honour to a gentleman of your cloth, entertained the gauger unawares. *Two!* I don't perceive that you carry a poke— don't be alarmed, it's only to put the joke in. *Three!*"

" Sir!" said my friend, haughtily, by no

means relishing Mr. Petrie's pleasantries, or sure of what hidden satiric meaning might lurk under that last periphrasis of the poke.

"Ha! ha! ha! ha!" laughed Mr. Petrie, heartily, "I thought I would be too much for you, Mr. Morland. I generally am for most people at first—know me better by-and-by. All wit, sir, pure wit, and nothing else. Lord bless you! we couldn't live without it here. I wonder Balph hasn't smoked us—again, you see! he's smoking his pipe in the garden. Not like Balph—nor the bottle either! Pop again. You see, sir, it can't be helped, and will out."

After their glass of tipple, he proposed that they should join his brother in the garden. "Balph," he observed, "sometimes falls asleep out of doors—at his age and habit of body not a good thing."

With the fraternal remark, much more to the purpose than his jokes, Logan thought, Mr. Petrie lifted the back door latch and stepped softly into the garden. .

As he anticipated, it was a mere jungle of the stunted undergrowth of the climate, the same that mantled the small rivulet winding along the garden foot, and at the further end of what purported to be a walk they found Mr. Balph, seated in a sort of arbour, smoking his meerschaum. He was half asleep. Awaking at the sound of his brother's voice, he looked up, recognised at once his late fellow-passenger, shook hands with Logan, and, making room for him on the seat, resumed the conversation exactly where they had left off on board the steamer. Logan noticed this the more particularly, as it was on the subject of parish schools. Mr. Petrie, who required but little sitting room, contrived to edge himself in also. And before he began his discourse, Logan being seated between the two brothers, facetiously compared himself to the device in the coat of arms over the front door, which, from the cursory glance he had time to take of it while in treaty with Mr. Petrie, appeared to be, in the centre, a tower, having for supporters an owl on the right and a lapwing on the left—emblems, the one of the *sapientia patriæ*, and the other of the winnowed sterility of its soil.

But after all, Parson Logan was not, perhaps, the man to sit in judgment here; the bent of his genius disqualified him for exploring the inner life of so singular a pair. Nay, their outer life was a mystery to him; what they found to do he could not imagine. The chief occupation of the elder brother seemed to be smoking tobacco in the willows, and the younger to inhabit the ancestral den. Of this latter he had an instance. Just as he was fairly getting into his subject, Mr. Petrie interrupted him with a sudden exclamation of alarm : " We've been lang enough out whatever. I must go and see what's gan on in the house ?" Now this, unless it was another joke, which it could hardly be, must have referred to the proceedings of a certain politic convocation of mice, who were believed to have a fine time of it in the parlour closet when they had the house to themselves.

Of Captain Kith's old acquaintance Balph appeared to know absolutely nothing beyond the bare fact that such a woman was his tenant, and that she had paid her first half-year's rent at Lammas, and although Petrie, indeed, appeared to be much fuller on the subject, his budget was conveyed with so many knowing winks, and inuendoes, and jocular and other vocabular obscurities, as defied all Logan's efforts to bring what the poor man said within anything like the bounds of reliable information.

To put the finishing touch to a lost day (for such my friend began to consider it), the Ruddocks were early people; dinner was over at the Hall, and the parson had to put up with bread-and-cheese; and as he had a person to see in the island about some other matter of business, he made no scruple of taking a somewhat abrupt leave. I did not know at the time, but I ascertained afterwards what Logan's business in Venturefair was. Effie having been made a present of a cow by Mrs. Deerness, he was over to see a man who was a famous maker of churns, milk bowies, and other such dairy gear. In short, his call at the Hall and his dairy purchases consumed fully a couple of hours, and it was nearly three o'clock in the afternoon when he returned to the public-house where he had left Captain Kith.

He saw the same woman who appeared to be landlady. She smiled in answer to his inquiries after the captain, and said she believed he was hiding somewhere about.

" I fancy I must have frightened the silly man away." And therewithal, fixing her dark melancholy eyes on the parson, she added, with another smile, " Your man, sir, and I are old acquaintances; you, I presume to conjecture, are the new clergyman lately come to Hallow ?"

A dry " Yes" from the parson.

" And the lady and you are as chief as may be, I suppose ?"

" Yes, we are on very good terms, or chief, as you call it."

The woman's face, as she still looked fixedly at him, seemed to fill with some strange and indescribable emotion.

" Tell her," she said, " tell the Lady of Hallow, when next you have speech of her, that you saw and spoke to Sally Baron."

" Your language is mysterious, my good woman," said Logan, " and would seem, if my ear does not deceive me, to intimate a grudge against an estimable lady and her family.   What mean you ?"

" The story is too long to tell, sir. Don't let me detain you from the worthy captain."

" You seem to be in poor circumstances," observed Logan.

" Yes, sir, I am very poor.   There's but

little money to be got in keeping a house like this."

" I was about to observe," continued my friend, " that you seem, in addition to your poverty, to be cherishing a frame and temper of mind that, believe me, are the worst seasoning ever was tried to improve a sorry lot."

" What you say, sir, is very true," replied the woman. " Poverty and the temper are two of the most difficult things to cure that I know."

" You appear, moreover, to have received a tolerably good education."

She interrupted him with a smile (if it was not dissembled) of much sweetness.

" You are young, sir, and romantic—pardon the freedom of the remark—but you must not go away with the idea that

you have discovered here to-day an in-
digent and reduced gentlewoman. I was
educated at a charity hospital, and as you
see, sir, I have not yet done with my
lessons."

Our parson, his compassion moved, said
here, with a kind of jocose earnestness,
" I warrant now, Miss Sally, were I to
offer you sixpence, you would fling it in
my face."

Logan put a shilling into her hand.

" Bless you, young man !" she said, with
some emotion. " Well, I am not what I
appear; once I was in very, very different
circumstances, but not now can I relate
my sad history. It may be that we shall
meet again, when perhaps you may hear my
story. Farewell, sir, for the present. You
will find Kith waiting for you down in
yonder shed on the shore."

It was even so. Directing his steps to-

wards the shed pointed out, he found Captain Kith beguiling the time after the
American fashion, with his knife and a
piece of wood. The captain's expressive
countenance wore in an unwonted degree the pale cast of thought. He liked
the captain, and was fond of drolling on
him.

" I have seen our landlady again, captain," said Logan, " and from all that I can
gather, she must have frightened you
wholly out of the house, and half out of
your wits."

" And time," said the captain, " with
her grusome questions, the upstart, tyrannical, and now forlorn castawa' besom! My
very flesh creepit, minister, to hear her at
her high English again, and her threaps
and her threats. It's an ald back story
now," continued the captain; " but when
she was in power across the way, and in

high favour with the leddy, there wasn't
a man, woman, or wean could call the
very duds that covered them their ain;
the very quinies durstna wear a new ribbon
at the kirk without Madam Sal's permis-
sion. Howanever, sir, you know, better
than I can tell you, the wicked shall not
be, and their place shall be cut off. Sae
the upshot was that Madam Sal was
found out at last. *And I had a hand in
that same,*" concluded the captain, somewhat emphatically, as well as abruptly.
He started up and led the way to their
boat, for once taking precedence of his
Reverence, a circumstance significant of
some passing mental disturbance in a man
so habitually observant of his proper
place.

Launching the punt, they put off on
their return passage. Lustily the captain
pulled out for the first half-mile or so, ere

he raised his oars to take breath and look about him, in the clear burning September afternoon; while the parson's gaze, directed backwards, was fixed on the deserted station and its miserable inn.

" I know not how it is, captain," said the parson, " but this woman, this Sally Baron, interests me. I cannot, as you would say, get her out of my head. Are you quite sure, my good friend, that there are not two sides to the story—that she had no provocation, no indifferent usage among you ?"

" I will not say that she had not," replied Captain Kith. " I ken few folk that ever suffered in this world—unless, with submission to your Reverence, it be the deil himself — but what could put in that plea. It's not," said the captain, growing positively oracular— "it's not the provocation, but the pride that comes of it, that pruvs fattle" (proves fatal). " This woman she was not of this country or degree, but came into it to pooss her fortune, as was thought; she would then be a gilpin of two or three and twenty. Her first beginning was with a family in Corbysholme as a who-ca'd, a better kind of bairn-maid."

" Governess," suggested Logan.

" That same," continued the captain. " Our present maister, that's now ald Hallow, was not then married, but a visiting bacheleer at most houses round about. In course, minister, I would tell this to nobody but yoursel'. Aweel, sir, the story went —be'd true be'd a leasing—that Hallow was gan to marry the governess. Whether there ever was anything in it, God kens; some said that there was, and that he let them laugh him out of her, and a freend's jeer is whiles hard to bide, as your reverence knows. Anyway, she was a vain, good-looking, hameless gilpin; and the master being, as I said afore, a bacheleer friend o' the house, he put nonsense in her head—that much was allowed on all hands —and the nobody-novice that she was, she expected to be made Leddy Hallow: she might as weel have expected to be Queen of Sheba! Ere lang, the maister married in his own sephere a wife, that's to say, our present honoured mistress; and Madam Sally, she gangs down to Dirdum and taks the first offer that cam to hand in her own sephere, a skipper and part owner of a trading brig to Leith, and the ports in the Furth of Forth. But fortune winna thraw, minister. Before the twelvemonth cam round, the proud besom's makshift marriage was coos'en up to her; she married

a plain seafaring man that she knew could
hardly sign his name, so the Lord sent a
storm, and man and vessel were never
more heard of. Not very long after that,
the laird heard of her as a widow, child-
less, and in very poorly circumstances;
and the leddy being like to tak the teeth
fever of Mr. Weatherby, the family doctor,
the same that's still in power, ald Brechin,
advised them to this woman for a nurse.
And that's how she cam amang us. But
I confess, your Reverence, it fickles me to
spell the fancy the leddy took to this
woman, this Sal Baron; howanever, beyond
dispute, a friendship it was, and it grew
great and strong, beyond all common
friendship in height, till the woman's head
was as high as Jack on the beanstalk, or
the gourd, your Reverence, of the prophet
Joppa!"

" Jonah, you would say, captain."

" The same, the same," quoth the captain; " he was on 's way down to Joppa, and I confounded the twa names. Howanever, that's nought to the story o' the woman. The ald story was not that so forgotten, your Reverence, but it whiles coost up ower the punch-bowl. Aweel, sir, if they had their joke, the laird had his answer. He just laughed and said, ' May none of them ever have a waur passing fancy at their board ends.' But it bred mischief in the end, your Reverence, and I canna help thinking was at the bottom of the hale dirdum. Great was her favour, but as great her downcome, and bitter and black, your Reverence, was the outcast between the leddy and her. But there was no particulars, not likely," concluded the captain; " ilka ane just shapet the story to their ain mind. She has not been heard of for many years, and a man I asked at, tells me she has been here about six months. Sae guess ye, minister, fat a carfuffle I gat at sight o' the name on that forlorn public-hoos. I wad it had looked in any airt but Hallow; it has a waesome glower."

"Once more, my dear captain, you are superstitious," said the parson. "You have told me the story of the downfal of an imperious favourite, and they are far from being few in this world. I will make inquiry into the poor creature's circumstances, and see what can be done for her."

And so ended the adventure of the day, the parson arriving at his own home in the evening in time for a cup of tea with Effie. Of Miss Sally Baron he judged it prudent to say nothing in the mean time. But he did Mr. Petrie Ruddock less than justice when he described his conversation as from beginning to end absolutely unintelligible—a mere glimmer and rush of words—a kind of hospitable convulsion. He did not say he expected, but it was possible that the other brother, Balph, who appeared to be the laird, might return his call.

CHAPTER XI.

LOGAN PREACHES HIS FIRST SERMON—A TWILIGHT SKETCH AT THE OLD PARISH CHURCH—WITH SOME ACCOUNT OF EFFIE'S TWO FIRST LOVERS.

SUNDAY brought a change of weather. When Effie looked out in the morning everything was shrouded in grey, and a chill wind moaning on the sea.

The absence of sunshine was considered rather a boon, however, by the principal personage of the day. To Mrs. Deerness, with her religious tendency to asceticism, the leaden solemnity of the atmosphere was pleasing and appropriate; it was, as it were, put on: and it was really with a heart full of maternal satisfaction that she said, "Now, boys, you are all to go to church."

A previous similar order had been issued to the inhabitants generally; but it needed not the feudal command to ensure a good muster among poor people to whom a sermon was become a double treat from its rarity. They came from the farthest parts of the island, and Logan had the satisfaction, supreme and dearest to the parsonic heart, of preaching to an overflowing audience. The text was, "I have brought you out of darkness into light." Verily this first sermon of our friend's was a shower in season after a long drought. The poor emptied hearts were filled again with something to talk about when they got home. If the preacher erred at all, it was towards the conclusion of his discourse, just before the final peroration, when he glanced more severely at the sin of Sabbath-breaking than the case at all warranted, or than he would have done on a wider acquaintance with their insular necessities.

They were asked to dine after at the house. Everything was in keeping; there was social enjoyment without that excess which sometimes disfigures the day of rest; and evening came clothed in the old conventional form (not the worst, perhaps), when those who had to go home went home, and all sat down to their books.

Logan having some sick calls to make at the Black Moss, Effie took the opportunity of indulging a fancy she had to see the old parish church, the gable and belfry of which, in the red twilight, reminded her of something she had seen very like it in a collection of sombre-coloured prints belonging to their father when they were children : this print haunted Effie's memory still, and often and regretfully had she endeavoured to trace back what had become of it.

The kirk of Hallow stands on the seaward verge of some high-lying downs, which, a little beyond, drop suddenly to the shore. Off this rocky coast there is good fishing, and when it begins to grow dark the natives may be seen in their small punts, each containing, generally, an old man and a boy ; in some cases you may find the little fellow alone, but rarely the old one, the climate and exposure to the weather rendering them more than usually torpid with years; and as it is their principal means of subsistence, they fish the whole or greater part of the night.

Observing these specks in the darkening twilight, Effie could not at first make out what they were; and to say the truth, she was a little shocked when she discovered, by watching attentively the nearest, that they were human beings, sitting in what could hardly be called boats, but a precarious kind of cobble, that looked as if it would fill and go down at every ripple. Nevertheless, Effie felt a keen interest in the poor creatures sitting out thus all night in the whistling wind, with perhaps a hundred fathoms water under them. On the whole, it did not continue to strike her that they were Sabbath-breaking, though that was one of the forms of the sin denounced in the day's sermon.

But the church. It was a small, plain Gothic building, with little to distinguish it from a common barn, except its single transept, lancet-headed windows, and belfry on the east gable. The windows were broken, the door was wide open, and the sea-breeze whistled through it, mingled with occasional dirge-like sounds as of singing, that seemed to come from the brood of cobbles below in the bay. But this, Effie thought, must be illusion; they could not be actual human tones which she heard—more likely they came from the bell being off the chain and swaying in the wind. Pulpit and pews of the rudest construction were overrun with fungus. "You never saw anything like it, Mary," wrote Effie; "the puddock-stools were growing on the very pulpit and book-boards, and some of the Bibles were lying about, just as they had been left since the last time it was preached in."

Shameful, shameful to see such a ruin! While Effie stood painfully entranced at the sight, suddenly she heard voices speaking outside, and, drawing back in some

alarm, she was greatly surprised to see old
Mr. Deerness enter the churchyard, accompanied by his eldest son, and followed
by a third person, a stranger to them,
apparently. The man appeared to be begging: so at least Effie inferred, from the
sharp, suppressed tone in which the
younger Deerness told him to go about
his business, and the elder's amendment
to give him sixpence put the matter beyond a doubt. The man got his sixpence
and disappeared, and she heard the Master, as if still chafing at the interruption,
say he was drunk, and the old man reply,
" Like enough."

Father and son walked round to the
side of the church fronting to the sea, and
Effie, without much thinking of the propriety or impropriety of the action, took a
peep at them from one of the windows.
They seemed to be looking for some par-

ticular gravestone. After considering the
ground attentively, old Mr. Deerness, in-
dicating two furrows with his staff, said,
"It should be here, or hereabout." The
Master then knelt down, and cleared
away the grass from both: at the second
he rose, and mechanically touched his
cap.

"You're sure?" said the father.

"Quite," replied the son. "The initials
and crest are plain enough."

"Then, so far we're at rest," said the old
laird; "I was in some doubts whether
the stone could be found, but I knew there
was one. Something else I had to say
to you, Melethor, for I plainly foresee
that when I am removed there is to be
strife between your mother and you, and
Raby——"

But here Effie caught herself, and got
as quietly out of the church as she could.

The incidents of the night were not yet ended. Kith, at the door, anxiously looking for them coming home, said there was a man in the parlour, " seekin to see minister, and she was dreed feared he was sair the warr o' drink !"

" Drink !" said Effie. " Oh, surely no."

" As sure as this is the Lord's night," said Kith.

Her mistress desired her to run for Miller Bisset, their neighbour, who, being luckily at home, was soon procured; then swiftly and silently returning with the miller they put him into the parlour. Now, the jolly miller was a soft-spoken young man of seventeen stone weight.

" That's a bonny afternoon been, freend," they heard the miller say; and again, no notice being taken of his first salutation, " If it's a fair question, wha or what may

you be, freend ?   Are you aware that this
is Sabbath night ?"

The man replied in hollow rub-a-dub,
evidently tipsy.

" Tell your master or your mistress my
name's Fletcher—do you hear ?—Gideon
Fletcher."

Gracious Heaven, Mary's brother !

Now, although Effie never greatly liked
this Mr. Gideon, still, having been an ad-
mirer when they first came to Chapel-end,
he was a sort of old flame, and such a shock
(coming tipsy on a Sunday night), after an
eighteen months' separation, was very,
very dreadful.   She ran at once for Logan.

But it was impossible to fortel what
view Logan would take of almost anything.
He came to the door of the house where
he was visiting—it was the last on his

list home—came out and heard Effie's
panting tale.

" You must be exaggerating, Effie," he
said; "you have been taken by surprise,
that's all. . It is impossible Fletcher can
be so altered, nor is it the least likely he
would have come to me had he been so
very much in drink—that part of it is
clearly an illusion of your own and your
messan Kith ; drink is always the first
thing women suspect. But come in—I
shall soon have done here."

Nearly an hour, however, was thus lost,
and when our parson reached his home for
the night Mr. Fletcher had been gone for
some time. Bitter were Logan's reproaches
on her cowardice, which had thus driven
" an old friend and brother in the ministry
to seek a night's lodging in the first hovel
that offered him the common rites of hospitality;" while Effie, a little nettled by so

much fine speaking at her expense, "daresay'd he would cast up in the morning." My friend looked as if he had a thrilling inclination to darraign some further battle with her upon that speech, but he forbore, out of respect to the night.

The gentleman did cast up in the morning. He looked very shabby and very sober, however that latter matter might have been; and if kindness could have atoned for a *late panic*, even the parson must have been satisfied with the reception accorded to his friend. But in truth it seemed very doubtful whether so drooping a plant could much benefit by any amount of watering, or how far natural gladness to see him could cheer so dull a guest. Fletcher was always a heavy fellow. What an account he gave of his missionary sufferings and doings!—labours he called them, but it was difficult to see their title to that designation; however, as Logan was in want of a helper—or fancied he was, which came to the same thing—the result was that he struck a bargain with Fletcher for a month.

The first day and the second passed off tolerably well—the new inmate accompanied Logan on his rounds; but the third day Mr. Gideon was ill and not able to go out; the fourth the same. Again Effie had to listen to the lachrymose story of his sufferings abroad. All day he talked of the ague, and kept up such a drone of that and his other climatic complaints, that, had he not been Mary's brother, Effie would have felt strongly tempted to ask him, " Man, man, are they all like you? for what a strange pit of dulness it must be!" In conclusion, he regretted his present impaired usefulness, and asked Effie to give him a glass of whisky. A whole day to ask a dram !

Logan heard her report with disapprobation. " What ! a clergyman, an invalid, and their guest, after all he had suffered for the spread of the Gospel, did she grudge the cheering stimulus of a glass of spirits in so clear a case of necessity?" He would not accuse her of positive insensibility—nervous tremors, the parson said —and pooh-poohed all her objections as foolish, frivolous, and worldly. " She had, moreover," he observed, " let slip the epithet ' ugly man,' as a further objection to his friend—and Fletcher was certainly no Adonis—but never let him hear such a word come out of her mouth again !"

The daily dram being thus carried by prescription, Effie heard less of the ague, and more and more of old times, of Roslyn

and Hawthornden, and sister Moll—in a
word, Gideon Fletcher did begin to show
symptoms of convalescence. Like a de-
cayed, but not altogether dead, shrub in
spring, there was even a feeble appearance
of blossom; and it was then that Effie's
other "braw wooer" appeared. I have only
to name Mr. Ruddock of Venturefair.

The parson was mightily pleased to see
his good friend Mr. Ruddock, and the
more so that Balph accompanied his first
visit by the gallant declaration that, "had
he known his good friend the parson had
such attractions to his peri ingle, he should
have been over long before now—by his
poat, he should!"

I need not say that Fletcher and he
fought like cats; and that Effie, if she was
not absolutely convicted of the fact, was
strongly suspected by the parson of giving

them abundance of that species of encouragement when his back was turned.

This, though an approximation, is not quite a fair statement of the case. But if they would fight, Effie could not help laughing. How could she? One day Balph departed the levee rather abruptly, with something like a distinct threat of formally calling his rival out. "If persons," he said, "would put themselves in opposition to gentlemen, they must take the consequences; he could see no reason why their cloth should protect them more as others. And by his poat he would not be long of being back again!"

Not long, indeed. Scarcely had he left the beach when Effie, who stood at the window watching her angry lover's retreating skiff, observed that he had put about and was paddling back to shore with

strokes of the utmost swiftness and fury.
Now, she knew, there was to be a battle;
and Effie retreated to the kitchen, where,
with Kith, she could watch it at safe distance—unless they should shut the parlour
door to it; which, however, they very
seldom did.

Balph re-entering the parlour, resumed
his seat in silence; he first knit his brows
on missing Effie, but instantly after looked
mightily pleased—it was a good sign finding his rival alone. Fletcher had taken
up a book; he continued to read on in
squalid and utter indifference to the presence of the Orcadian magnate; while
Balph Ruddock on his side directed a bale-
ful and searching glance at his irrespective
competitor. "Confound the fellow," said
Mr. Ruddock to himself, "he takes my
return tamt coolly!"

A new and alarming light began to

strike the bearded solitary. What if the man was a cousin, or something of that advanced sort? At length he asked him.

" Ahem!" said Balph, "if I might teek such a liberty as to—a—pree, sir, are you any reletion to the house?"

" None," answered the bookworm.

" Then what, pree," quoth Balph, "in the name of common civility? Don't you know it is not that book you are gnawing at, but my—my heart! Man of sighs, I charge you to declare yourself! What is to be the end of all this?"

Fletcher raised his dull, yellow eyes for a moment, surveyed his lairdly rival, blew a sigh in his face, and fell again to his book. It was the one solitary advantage Fletcher had over him, and poor Mr. Ruddock's want of "the lair," as it has been emphatically termed, shot through his heart with a pang unutterable.

Still he was Ruddock of Venturefair.

"Perhaps," said Balph, highly nettled, "as you seem to be the downdie here (the reader must not forget what a downdie is)—perhaps you will have the civility to carry a mess'ge to the young leedy, and tell her that I am——"

Fletcher rose with a yawn, and walked out.

"Here!" shouted Balph after him, "the unmannerly, tamt, miserable beast, he does not know common civility! Surely, to Heaven's goodness, she will never take such a sluggard as that. But she's a pratty girl, and I am determined. Yes, I am determined to give Petrie the surprise I was preparing for the best of brothers."

There are a great many worthy and deserving men in the world, who are not to be despised because they happen to be a little ridiculous; Mr. Ruddock was one of them. Why should not Effie become Mrs. Balph Ruddock?

In the mean time, an invitation from Mrs. Deerness to spend a week at the House, gave her a short respite from both her admirers.

CHAPTER XII.

DEATH OF THE OLD LAIRD.

NONE of the family, not even Mrs. Deerness herself, seemed to have any apprehen-
sion that the event was so near. The night
he died (the second or third of Effie's visit),
an incident occurred that struck her afterwards as in some sort a precursor of the
event. It was early in the evening before
tea; the boys were in the schoolroom
opposite the parlour, or what had been the
schoolroom before their tutor was paid off.
It was used as a smoking and billiard

room now, and hitherto there had been no interdict on the run of amusements and their meeting in it as usual; the old man at the fireside was accustomed to hear them knocking the balls about—it was part of his evening as well as theirs—and Mrs. Deerness, with all her ideas of propriety and impropriety, was loth (how loth!) to proclaim silence just yet.

Like lads of their age they had their occasional bits of squabbles. Mr. Wea₊therby and Mr. Jerrold in particular were noted for carrying on the braggadocial war, and out of that arose the incident referred to. In general this single-stick wit was confined to the limits and rules of the game, but on this occasion some heat appeared to have been engendered, and the altercation was not exclusively limited to words; there was a scuffle, as near an approximation to blows as might be between brothers, and Mr. Jerrold, his voice angry, sharp, and raised, and sufficiently audible in the parlour, called Mr. Raby "Lugs' Heir."

Effie had once or twice heard her brother speculating on what might be the import of this mysterious title : that it was offensive she understood, and of this there was present proof; in an instant Mrs. Deerness was in the schoolroom, quelling her turbulent brood, and if they were not greatly mistaken in the sounds that reached the ear, they were bound to conclude that the offender was undergoing something like a cuffing at the maternal hand for having used this forbidden epithet. Miss Deerness blushed scarlet. But what Effie chiefly noticed was the effect on the old man at the fireside ; he answered any little question that was put to him, but never voluntarily spoke from the occurrence of the above incident to his going to bed. At his usual hour of nine o'clock he rose and walked up-stairs.

His departure was rather felt than observed; at the vingt-et-un table there was a general pause, and Mrs. Deerness, who was reading the *Witness*, laid aside her paper.

" I don't think your father's so well tonight, boys," she said, coming forward to the card-table.

And the Master remarked that he had forgot to say good night. " I think, mother," he added, " that you should send for the doctor."

She answered, " Oh no, he's not so ill as that, Melethor! You surely don't think him so ill as that ?"

" I do. My father is very ill," said the Master.

"But it is such a night," she still urged; "it is impossible to send. I don't think you could get anybody to go."

The doctor lived in Corbysholm. There was some talk among the boys of going for him notwithstanding, but the long, loud roll of the night without silenced them. The Master walked up-stairs to his father's room, and on his return said he thought him looking a little better.

At eleven they went to bed. Effie slept with Harriet. The young girl, who had been running about all day, was soon asleep, and so was spared the pang till all was over. Effie, anxious and apprehensive, was still sitting up when the cry arose; and such a cry! it rang through the whole house. "Melethor, come here! come here! Oh, boys!" Effie ran to the room. In such a summons all seemed to be included.

Mr. Deerness, partly undressed, appeared to have fallen from his chair while sitting talking to Mrs. Deerness. His son was lifting him up—at the same time as if keeping off his mother. Her "Oh! he's not gone!" was heartrending. The rest of his sons came rushing in, and they laid the old man on his bed; the servants, too, were by this time in the room, and the first thing cried for was the doctor. The clatter down stairs for the doctor was the most appalling sound of its kind Effie had ever heard.

The women only now remaining, Mrs. Deerness, said: "Oh, will none of you run for Annie Gatehouse till the doctor comes?" Annie Gatehouse, the old woman at the lodge, long a servant in the house, was usually consulted on occasions of distress. They ran accordingly for Annie. "Annie," said Mrs. Deerness, as if eager to take the first word, "your master has had a fainting-fit, and we have sent for the doctor. I expect him every moment."

Annie Gatehouse went straight to the bed, put her hand on the brow, tried the dropped jaw, and then said aside to the women, "Get her oot o' here; a doctor's of nae use here."

"What's that you say, Annie? Oh no, he's not gone; it canna be—he was speaking to me as well as ever he was in his life when——" She seized the hand of the corpse and kissed it passionately, and then she looked at the face: they had covered it with a linen cloth: she tore it off.

But this was not all—the doctor? They were now as afraid to pronounce the name as they had been clamorous before. There were lights running to and fro down at the haven, all the boatmen of the place were on the quay, and the Master and his brethren. Melethor said, "This is a terrible night to ask you to put out in, men, but which of you will go for the doctor to my father? Rent free," he added; that is, whoever went should have their small farms rent free for life. The men all protested their willingness to go if the thing were possible, but no boat, they said, could have a chance in such a night. Again the Master spoke : "It is quite clear that we" (referring to his brothers) "cannot *all* go. Which of you will go with me for the doctor?" Of the boatmen only Captain Kith and old Hoolie volunteered; of his brethren, William Institute was the first, and him he took. The boat was launched amid a clamour of dissuasion, and they were gone.

Meanwhile Effie, as soon as she could get away, taking one of the servants with her, hastened down to the haven, hoping that she might yet be in time to prevent their putting to sea. But the lapse of time was greater than she supposed; they had been gone half an hour; and Effie and her companion, Lizzie Scale, sat down on the log seat under the kelp shed wall, afraid to return to the house.

A beacon fire had been kindled on the point of the pier; its reflexion flared out on either side of the foaming waves, leaving all in front black as the darkest cavern, and to the two crouching women seemingly as stony still; Effie felt as if the howling of the wind were confined to the point of the pier where the people were assembled, hovering in and out about the fire. But little intelligence could be gleaned from their gestures; in general the countenances of the men expressed deep and terrible, but not hopeless, anxiety.

Effie dreaded how it would be. A loud gust of wind roared over the house, and the writhing woman sat up and listened for a second or two; all restraint was now snapped like a thread. Mrs. Deerness became quite unmanageable; she broke loose from the dead old man and the terrified women. Her first exclamation as she swept past, the flutter of her dress in the wind striking Effie sharply on the face, was, "Oh, boys, are you all here!" When the truth was made known to her, she struck herself with both hands on the face. The scene is not to be described.

At that moment of distraction one of the men stationed on the outlook reported that he saw a light; he was confirmed by another; and Effie herself, shaded by the wall from the flare of the beacon fire, distinctly saw it for a moment like a red spark. But was it not merely a spark from the fire? No. The man reported it again. But in the black distance it was impossible to say how far the light might be out.

At this crisis Effie was almost startled (if anything could have startled one in such a scene) by a most extraordinary demonstration of filial tenderness and fraternal energy on the part of Mr. Weatherby: himself in all human probability now the laird, he implored his mother (how odd the term mamma sounded in such a coil) to allow him to launch another boat to the rescue—and, indeed, he did seem to make some attempt—his voice was heard above all the Babel of tongues. But somehow it came to nothing. The man on the look-out reported the light again, and instantly the clamour was stilled. As before, it was seen only for a moment, but this time, from the increased size as well as ray of the light, it was visibly much nearer—inside the deep water line—within, as it were, their very grasp almost, men and women, mistress and dependents, all huddled together at the brink.

Now was the time for old Pan Whittet, the smuggling old landlord of the Haven public-house, to relieve the agony of suspense by a sage remark. "If she swamps with them now," said Whittet, a pedantic old man-of-war's-man, "they can swim it! All—unless it be the doctor; and perhaps *he* may pike up an oar."

At length Jerrold the Jollyboat, with a loud bellow that sounded almost like laughter, cried out, "There they're!" and Effie sprang forward just in time to see the sight. The light of the beacon fell upon the backs of the rowers, stripped to their shirts and stretching to their oars, and on

the thin, bent figure of the old doctor in the
stern-sheets steering, with the lantern between his knees. One stroke of the oars
gave them thus to view, each individually
distinct, the Master pulling the bow oar,
Captain Kith and old Hoolie the two
middle, and William Institute the after;
and the next flung them upon the beach,
the boat half full of water. As they
jumped out, the bystanders gave one shout
of acclamation for the living laird, and
almost before he could ask the question,
" My father?" all again was silence for
the old one that night departed.

The heroism of her two sons melted Mrs.
Deerness, and now she wept freely and
naturally, with none of the overstrained
and terrible agony of grief she had before
exhibited. But the young men themselves
turned their backs on their fruitless feat
with a cold indifference amounting almost

to thanklessness for their escape—with a slight exception, if it could be called such, a little peevish explosion of temper on the part of William Institute. "Too late," said he, "it's hard, whatever!"*

"I knew we would be," said the Master —"I knew it all along."

And this was the fact. From the moment he lifted up the old man, Melethor Deerness knew that his father was dead, but he acted on the first and last impulse of the moment, the bare possibility, namely, that it might be a case of suspended animation. He merely added, grasping the old physician's hand, "I am sorry, doctor, we have given you so much trouble;" and the mournful procession which closed one dynasty of the house of Hallow and opened a new left the haven.

* "Whatever" for "however" is a peculiar idiom in Orkney not altogether confined to the uneducated.

As for our poor Effie, all of her heart
that was left unbroken by the death of old
Mr. Deerness, to whom she was much
attached, was given to the four who had
braved such a night to recover him, to the
Master and William Institute, Captain
Kith and old Hoolie; and it took a time to
recover her ordinary calm tone of mind,
undisturbed by the recollection of the four
stretched to their oars. The symmetry of
the young men, contrasted with the burly
forms of the older boatmen, awoke in Effie
all the hitherto dormant springs of romance. It was well for her that she had
some good sense to fall back upon.

CHAPTER XIII.

THE FUNERAL—WITH SOME AFTER-BURIAL REFLECTIONS AND
ILLUSTRATIONS.

THE sort of burial service which the
practice of many of our Scottish clergy has
substituted for the solemn ritual which the
Church of England has appointed for the
rendering of dust to dust, varies according
to circumstances, the wishes of parties, or
the will and opinions of the clergyman
officiating. The most common-place form
is to read a chapter and pray before a small,
select, and specially invited company in the

house; comparatively few think of praying at the grave, and, indeed, where this is left to extempore inspiration, there are many cases in which it had better be pre-termitted, at least *there;* and there are still a good many who, adhering to the rigid model of no service at all, hold solemn silence to be the best ritual.

The funeral was large—the largest Effie had ever seen. From the neighbouring islands, as well as from the more distant mainland, parties came to pay the last tribute to the old laird. Caldwel Gil-christ was there, not without an eye to the shaken supremacy of the Church on an occasion calling for ghostly comfort to afflicted relatives. So, also, was Mr. Cal-throp (old Crawtaes); it is not said whether he was invited. Logan, who here saw his reverend antagonist for the first time, thought he looked *incog.*, and, at the same time, anxious to get in his hand. There was a restlessness and a flushed look of nervous anxiety about him, Logan said; his shabby black gloves were out at the fingers, his black suit was dirty and worn to an extreme that might have argued actual poverty; altogether there was a general expression of moral indigence. And his physiognomy, so far as he could judge, was that of a man sullen and resentful, and watching his opportunity.

For anything that is known to the contrary, there might be some truth in this theory of Logan's. The old Residuary, numbered with the common crowd at the grave, very likely did feel something shorn of his former respect; as regards his gloves and garb, generally, these were only part and parcel of the man. I forget whether Professor Teufelsdroch touches precisely upon the point or not, but this is one of the commonest freaks in the whole history of clothes, namely, that while it is the gay nature of the majority to cast them, there are always here and there some who, out of a deep-rooted slovenliness or sullen sorrow, can no more part with their old clothes than they can give up their old habits.

The whole thing, however, was simply a conjecture of my friend's. No unseemly altercation occurred to disturb the sad and solemn rite of rendering dust to dust, which generally suspends party animosities for the time, and, were it a little more deeply considered, would go far to suspend them altogether. If both reverend gentlemen came, as it is just possible they did, expecting the preference, they were disappointed — neither of them was asked to pray either in the house or at the grave: they were observed, when it came to *that*,

to ruffle up and to press nearer to the
Master ; but there was something dangerous in his eye that told them a quarrel
over his father's remains would not be
tolerated. And thus, in the presence of
his people and of the women and children
at every door within sight, standing at the
doors in the sun, was the old laird en-
tombed without a prayer, by the vast and
silent multitude inwardly conning to
themselves his great hospitality, his rough
old-world sensibility and goodness, and
many other great departed merits. It is
said that Markus Skeldar blubbered; but
this wants confirmation.

" How soon are the dead forgotten !"
has long been a favourite complaint. In
general it means nothing; a morbid expression not intended to have any meaning : one of those bottom bubbles in our
nature that burst when they rise to the

surface. Sometimes, however, you hear
the sentence spoken in the way of graver
accusation by the advocates of the worth-
less supremacy. In this shape it is one of
those convenient parasites to the doctrine
of man's supreme and utter degradation :
indeed, it would be idle to expect these
gentlemen not to make the most of so
capital a case against us as our notoriously
proven readiness to desert the dead. They
have discovered our weak side here; they
have discovered that the act of burial is
attended with a sensible though secret
feeling of relief to surviving relatives—to
all present, indeed. They have discovered
this sweet little secret of nature : no wonder that we return so soon to the vanities
and enjoyments of life as if nothing had
happened ! They have discovered—well,
the truth is, we *are* careless sinners—
nothing will stop, nothing arrest us; and

the gentlemen's notions of the dead, to say nothing of the living, are a credit to them.

At dinner, Caldwel Gilchrist talked of their bereavement like a man inspired, clearly and fully, and, as he believed, to the entire conviction of the young men, deducing from their sire's departure the saving doctrine of conformity, and their duty to their parent Church, at present also in circumstances of mourning and affliction. At dinner, Markus Skeldar talked lugubriously, like a half-drowned sinner, of his oyster-beds and other suspended worldly amusements and occupations. Which of these two had the old man most in remembrance?

At the manse, as there was no dinner in respect of the occasion, the minister had to get his tea a little earlier. I know not what wandering white cloud it was

that came over Effie—came up sailing out
of the far back past.   In the very midst of
their meal, in the midst of her brother's
brooding, she suddenly gave way to a most
unauthorised fit of light-hearted reminis-
cence, respecting a certain jaunt (to take
tea at their Aunty May's) which they had
performed when they were children, under
the auspices of old Saunders of the Salt-
market and his laughter-loving dame, in
which the parent pair were so happily contrasted to the life; Saunders stalking along
in the covenant, his features relaxed into
a smile of grim approbation; their mother
Nelly gathering flowers and butterflies for
them, the very type of worldly vanity. All
this, I say, Effie poured out with such a
sudden sunny life-likeness, that Logan,
startled out of his theological train of
thought, amazed and horrified, thought

Effie must certainly be possessed by the devil.

" Effie," said he, when he had in some degree recovered from his astonishment, " if that is all the respect you have for the memory of your own parents, you might, at least, pay some to a day so solemn in the annals of these islands."

Which of these two was most at one with the deceased laird? their sire Saunders, and their mother Nelly?

CHAPTER XIV.

CRAWTAES ASSERTS HIS RIGHT TO PREACH THE LAIRD'S FU-
NERAL SERMON, AND GIVES NOTICE OF HIS INTENTION TO
THAT EFFECT.

IT would be a mistake to suppose that Mr. Calthrop was all this while sitting callously at his ease, joking as heretofore to his beadle, John Gilbroddie. Far from it. Restless, tossed about from one course to another, with a character in reverend rags, so to speak, assailed by the remembrance of past derelictions and a stigma put upon his name, no hope, no mercy, from either private or public opinion, the death of Mr. Deerness decided the question at a blow, and recovered the old Residuary to his duty. He went home from the funeral, and wrote as follows to the umquhile Master, now the laird :

"DEAR SIR,—I beg to intimate that it is my intention, D.V., and weather permitting, to preach in Hallow next Lord's-day, in connexion with the present mournful occasion, the decease, namely, of your respected and lamented father. In making this intimation, I may also take leave to express my regret that, owing to the recent unhappy divisions in the Church, such intimation is more formally necessary now than it was used to be. I will not deny that I may have been something remiss—age and infirmity seldom mend the natural indisposition to contend with the elements—but in future, weather at all permitting, I shall be across every alternate Sabbath, when I trust to have the pleasure of seeing yourself and people as usual.   Accept of my sincere condolence in the present family bereavement, and believe me

" Yours sincerely,

" ROBERT CALTHROP."

To this the Master, as he was still occasionally called, returned the following answer :

" DEAR SIR,—I have received your note, and beg to thank you for the tribute of respect you would pay to your friend my late father's memory.   Excuse me if I take the liberty to observe that the custom of preaching what are called funeral sermons has always appeared to me one that would be more honoured in the breach than the observance. Theologically, my father was not a subject for pulpit eulogy, and, to be perfectly frank with you, I really don't see what you could make of it. We all know that he was a good man, but it is painful to the delicacy of friends and relatives to be told so publicly.

"With regard to your resuming your ministrations here, while nothing would have given me greater pleasure, I must frankly again tell you there are insuperable objections in the way. The new section of the Church has established here a resident pastor; my mother, my sister, and I believe I may add, my brothers, have all given in their adherence, and, so far as I can judge, the people are pleased; so that, all things considered, the outlying field and domestic objections, I hope you will see it to be more for the dignity of your character to abstain from a course which can be productive of little good, and must give rise to no end of dissension. What the ultimate result of this movement may be is another question; what I would entreat of you to see in the mean time is, that the observance of the Sabbath being provided for, your attendance is not necessary, and any interference at present would be impolitic until the ferment is over.

" Believe me to remain, dear sir,

" Faithfully yours,

" MELETHOR DEERNESS."

This drew the following rejoinder from the old gentleman :

" DEAR SIR,—Many thanks for your advice to me to play the part of Blind Hookie with a view to the dignity of my character ! As a means to an end, I can only say that I differ with you. In the remarks with which you have been at the trouble to favour me, it is obvious that you start from the common point of view, namely, that, as a body, we have somehow forfeited all ecclesiastical status and title to respect; and, moreover, that so long as our temporals are safe, that is all we care for. Permit me to say, a more vulgar mistake was never entertained—a more malicious aspersion was never propagated by men calling themselves brethren. I have been minister of Hallow a long time now, nearly forty years before these fanatics were ever heard of, and I shall certainly continue to do my duty without the slightest regard to them or their arrangements. But I should for ever sincerely regret should a little dereliction on the one hand, arising, as before said, from age and infirmity, and a brush of windy zeal on the

other, be the means of driving your respected family from the house of God to
worship in this temple made with hands;
as I shall no less also sincerely deplore
should any *domestic dissensions* arise there-
from. In the mean time, my duty is clear;
there are many of the humbler members of
my flock who I know will be glad to see
me again. Repeating my former intimation, that I shall, D.V., preach at the usual
hour on Sabbath next, I have to request
that you will cause promulgation of the
same to be made according to the use and
wont practice of the combined parish of
Corbysholm cum Hallow. And I remain,

" Dear sir, yours sincerely,

" ROBERT CALTHROP."

Caldwel Gilchrist was still at Hallow
when this conclusion of the correspondence
came to hand. It was rowed across the

Frith by Mr. Calthrop's beadle, and delivered to the young laird as he was taking
a turn along the beach with his reverend
kinsman. He read, and then handed the
letter to Caldwel with a bitter laugh. Mr.
Gilchrist coloured a little; he read the
note, however, with his habitual com-
posure, and then observed, somewhat
austerely, " I see nothing in it to laugh
at."

" You don't ?" said Melethor; " why, it.
is enough to make the * * * * * laugh !
You don't mean to say you believe that
the sudden revival of this wrong-headed
old original has been effected by a sense
of duty, as he chooses to put it—a man
who for forty years has habitually neglected his duty ?"

" Indeed do I, my dear Melethor," replied the calm and imperturbable churchman. " In the language of a zealot, and ad-

dressed to a zealot, the case, as you put it, might, indeed, appear overwhelming; but add a drop or two of common sense to lay the froth, and let us see what it really comes to."

Admire, gentle reader, this distinguished and reverend chemist, with the cup of the case in one hand, and the bottle of common sense in the other. Take a clear view of him, adding the precise number of drops required to lay the froth. It is unnecessary to quote the speech at full length. The reverend gentleman observed, in conclusion :

"There is no essential difference, then, between the Residuaries, as they affect to stigmatise us, and these excited, and, as they fancy themselves, triumphant deserters, unless it be in their present arrogant pretensions. To come, then, to the case. Calthrop, I admit, is not the most model

man in our Church; he has some habits
which it would be desirable to see modified, but of that there is no hope—he is of
the old school. Still, he is a good man in
the main ; he has been, as he reminds you,
forty years minister here; and he is attached
to your family, the more, perhaps, that,
being an old bachelor, he has no ties of
his own. Can you wonder, then, at his
making the present stand? I know nothing
of the young man on the other side, but I
question whether he has the talents and
general good sense and piety of our poor
old friend. And do not you, my dear sir,
be misled by the vulgar notion that the
Church of Scotland is extinct, because a
sudden explosion of domineering and de-
feated ecclesiastical ambition has drawn off
half her numbers. On these grounds I
say, and say it emphatically, give Calthrop
another chance."

Melethor readily assented to this moderated view of the old gentleman's shortcomings. "Nay, more," he added, "so far as I am personally concerned, I have no hesitation in owning that I am with you at heart."

"Now God bless you for that word, my dear Melethor," interjected Caldwel Gilchrist, warmly.

"Yes," continued the other, "it is not difficult to see what will be one notable point in the new constitution, addressed, as they phrase it, to the hearts and consciences of men. I have no notion of surrendering my right of private judgment to any religious association whatever. Look you, Caldwel, that has been always, less or more, the clutch of you all: wriggle in that like; I will sit down in the way of fellowship with any body of professing Christians, but to the tyrannical combination of any who must have our minds all of one brand, as they mark sheep, I will not submit."

"Surely," observed Mr. Gilchrist, a little ruefully, however, "perhaps it is to be lamented that a popular creed and the right of private judgment have never yet been reconciled. Dealing in conflicting mysteries as we do (of course this is strictly confidential), I have sometimes had dawning visions of the possibility of such a state of things. But I think we come nearest it as matters at present stand."

"You do. You can appeal to time as an ecclesiastical government, let the other side take fright, call you the valley of dry bones, and run and rant at you till they are tired. Your despotism was not a prying despotism; old, it was friendly to meditation and private thought. Thus your shade was felt to be grateful, and some piety was found growing under it. But there was not enough of it, I suppose, or the peace of the religious world had lasted too long; or, at any rate, by hook or by crook, they must go to war. In their own phrase, they groaned to be delivered. One man talked to another, and the notion of coming to a stand with the state spread as rapidly as a strike among the mill hands of Manchester. At last 'Empty' was pronounced upon you, and in at the rent the gust came, leaving the Church a ruin, only not entirely deserted. Whether it may not eventually be the better for the blast, remains to be seen. In the mean time, we have got this religious republic ushered in with joy and rejoicing, and gladness on every side; with spiritual freedom for its motto, and a code

that practically comes to this: large
donations, large observance, the hundred
points of orthodoxy; and that all these
may be rigidly enforced, and freedom, full,
perfect, and complete, secured, universal
tyranny over the right of individual
opinion. This will, no doubt, produce a
good deal of piety of a kind; but the
piety which is chiefly remarkable for its
vulgar abundance, and is notoriously
known to chuckle over its spread; that
makes men neither better nor wiser, nor
more thinking than they were before—for
thinking according to prescription is no
thinking at all; that contributes nothing
to the general improvement of social
morality but the old suspicion of good
works, and leaves good taste, and not un-
frequently charity, to shift for themselves,
and all this depending on the Mammonish

impetus of money contributions, *may* turn up a happier and a better world by-and-by, but it is not just at present. I don't, therefore, blame Calthrop for following his instincts — sense of duty he calls it. What I find fault with is his wrong-headed obstinacy, that will not yield to the clear necessity of a particular case. Had Hallow been his only field, I could have excused him, but with Corbysholm to recover the lost ground in (and it is more than he can overtake), what but sheer perversity should bring him across here when I have told him (and he knows) the discord that will be the consequence?"

" Stay," said Mr. Gilchrist, introducing the pause persuasive, at the skilful use of which, in argument, few could match him; " are you sure, my dear Melethor, that the premise of your argument is quite sound ?

This discord hypothesis of yours, is it not merely a manifestation of your own peculiar idiosyncrasy—a chimera, in short? I have long noticed this to be a tenet peculiar to your mind. You set out with the foregone conclusion that all *theological* attempts to settle the differences of the religious world must necessarily end in failure and discord. A grievous error, believe me. Without a theological basis there can be no religion; take away that, and religion would evaporate in sentiment, a sort of marsh mist arising from the minds of the fanciful and sensitive few."

" Had we time," said the new laird, doggedly, " or could it serve any good, I would make bold to dispute that proposition, Caldwel, my boy."

" Of course you would, my dear Melethor, and disprove it too; but do not, in a

serious conversation like this, call me
' Caldwel, my boy.' "

" Very well, then, I won't, Mr. Gilchrist.
A theological basis of religion is one thing,
and an everlasting theological contention
and defiance of everything like basis, of
the very idea of basis, in another. Have
you not the Bible ? Is it not written, Love
God and your neighbour? Why this
enormous and complicated web for ever
spinning and never done, as if that were
necessary to catch the minds of men ? I
don't care one farthing, Mr. Gilchrist, for
your horrified looks. I tell you the blind
assent, the piety you sow and are content
to reap, is not religion, nor anything like
it. You cast your eyes proudly to heaven,
as if you would say, *Look yonder, have we
not filled it !* I see only an enormous and
far spun out intervention of theology,
filled, indeed, with human minds, or what

once were human minds; and I see other
shadows creeping about that have some
resemblance to yourselves, the spinners, to
whom it has become a second nature. But,
unless it be yourselves, can you point in
these days to a single living instance worth
the catching, those struggling to get out
of it not counting? And why all this?
Shall I tell you my notion of the reason
why?"

" Do," said the priest of Stifbakness.
" I find, Melethor, that I am ignorance
itself in your hands. Do. I mightily
long to be informed."

" Nay, now you are angry, Caldwel.
But you are not to run away with the idea
that I am an infidel because I stick up for
my reason. There are mysteries I do not
comprehend, but they do not shock me as
I find them in the Bible; they only shock
me when a body, professing to be teachers

of the Book, according to their tradition-
ary and clerical conceptions of the whole,
manufacture them into downright contra-
dictions, and for the evident purpose of
laying on a nonsense-tax to keep the upper
hand of my mind. I'll stick to the Bible
as I'll stand to my life, the two are all we
have; but I'm not to be told that this
means that and that this."

The churchman, however, was determined to win. "The old story, my dear
Melethor—the old story of priestcraft.
Your theory of a simplified creed in which
there shall be no complexity, no subject-
ing of the individual mind to the *mass*, no
abasement of self, no trial of the faith, no
wrangling, and in one word no suffering, is
simply a Utopian dream, an amiable infi-
delity of which you will see the unsound-
ness when you have lived a little longer."

"Will I?" said Melethor, interrupting

the avalanche for a moment. " I know the mass better. Your Protestant predilections have carried you rather too papal lengths there, Mr. Gilchrist !"

It cost the descending churchman a tremendous effort to proceed, but he succeeded, and thus went on :

" I am astonished that you do not even now perceive the radical defect in your argument. Your notion of simplifying the Incomprehensible in preference to symbolising as *we* humbly endeavour to do, is *primâ facie* a logical impossibility, carrying absurdity in the face of it, because it presupposes a religious spontaneity or power in the human mind which does not exist."

" So you tell the old wives.—But here comes Whittet with a bargain of fish."

CHAPTER XV.

CRAWTAES PREACHES HIS FUNERAL SERMON, AND AFTERWARDS
DINES AT THE HOUSE—OLD ASSOCIATIONS, THOUGH DISAP-
PROVED, NOT EASILY OBLITERATED.

HAVING some doubts of the new laird's
complying with his edict, Mr. Calthrop
sent over John Gilbroddie, his beadle, to
see it enforced, and to make proclamation
in his name. "And see, buddo,"* said
the old gentleman, "that thou dinna spare

* Buddo is an Orkney expression of endearment, somewhat
equivalent to the Shetland jarto.

the bell this time. I nominate and commissionate and send thee forth, buddo, even as the Boroughstown bellman on the mainland is sent out by the magistrates to cry fresh fish."

The proclamation that there would be sermon as usual in the old place of worship occasioned a very general dilemma. On Saturday, Captain Kith came with a petition to the Master—for so he was still more frequently called. It seemed to be a point of delicacy towards Mrs. Deerness to continue the subordinate title until the expiration of the period of mourning.

" It was just," said the captain, " these peri anxious bodies, sir, about the morn; they're in grit distress, more specially the ald carles. They was minded, sir, to see yoursel' about it if you would gang and speak to them."

" Surely, Kith; where are they ?"

"You're sure, sir, you'll na be angry," said the ambassador. "They're dreed ill, and there's mair nor a pickle o' them—a hunder, maybe, or thereawa. They're down, ald and young, wi' their best Sabbath-day's claes on, at the Dead Pool o' Drapness."

The spot selected by the islanders for a meeting with their young laird was one of those fissures peculiar to these rocky, isolated coasts. They do not in general penetrate very far, but this of Drapness in Hallow is of considerable extent, — a narrow rent, enclosing between black rocks a deep, dismal gulf fringed with just a strip of shore of the same sable hue. I take the more notice of this, that subsequent events in the story have given an additional interest to the locality.

It was here, then, in this "cleft of the

rock," that the people met their landlord, and expressed their desire of going to church in the use and wont place in honour of the deceased master; the petition concluded with a hope that the young laird would stand between them and the consequences. Melethor bit his lip at this sufficiently broad though covered allusion to his mother, but he felt it would have been a sin against fellow-feeling to take offence. He replied, in a short speech, that there could be no consequences in a matter so entirely at their own disposal. All were at liberty, he said, to indulge the sentiment who felt it; still, it was but recalling a shadow according to an old custom, the use or good of which might be doubted; therefore, others were equally at liberty to adhere to the new communion who thought proper. And having thus far hinted his mind on their common dilemma, he left the quotum to be adjusted by Captain Kith, devoutly hoping our friend Logan would not have to preach to empty pews.

On the Sunday morning, when she understood that her son was going to hear old Crawtaes (as a duty he owed to his father's memory), Mrs. Deerness had one of her fits—so Effie called them, and perhaps the name is as significant as any other we could find. " What!" she exclaimed, " do you call an Erastian hash from a perjured stipendiary of a perjured state divine service?—a sermon according to the Gospel of Christ?—an honour to your father's memory? Do you call a disgrace and a profanation——"

Without greatly diminishing the numbers at Logan's, there was a tolerable attendance at the old parish church; and when the reverend delinquent took his seat in the pulpit he did not behold altogether without emotion so many of the old familiar faces.

The reader must already have formed some idea of this gentleman. Robert Calthrop of Corbysholm (better known as Crawtaes) was one among the knots of reverend topers who in that day, when they got together, were absolutely scandalous, and whose orgies alone, had there been no other cause, were enough to have alarmed the sober, and to have led to a general reformation. It is curious to observe this characteristic distinction still between the abstemious pastors of the new denominations and the moderated potations of the worthies of the old. The original drunkards have died out; it was

necessary that they should; I doubt
whether one of them (genuine) could be
found in all Scotland now, but in 1843
there were not a few still alive who suffered all the horrors of that revolution.*

On this category was Robert Calthrop,
the toper and wit of a by-past generation,
left with nobody to joke with but his
beadle, or to get mellow with at all; all
gone but himself. Calthrop was an old
bachelor. A man of considerable though
uncultivated powers and unbounded vulgar
humour; possessing more natural eloquence
and real ability than for example the
polished Caldwel Gilchrist, and a better
preacher than our friend, though Logan

---

* I remember, when I was a lad, of being present with my
father at a funeral symposium, or "dirgie," where the company, except ourselves, were all clergymen, five in number.
I have seen some jolly drinking bouts since, but nothing com-
parable to that.

had made all the best modern models his study.

The old man's homely colloquial style was well adapted to his subject. His text was from the Psalms. " Thou carriest them away as with a flood; they are as a sleep: in the morning, they are like grass which groweth up. In the morning it flourisheth, and groweth up; in the evening it is cut down, and withereth."

There is a common opinion that this sort of thing does not require much capacity; any young preacher with a little warmth of feeling can do it; and undoubtedly so any young preacher can after his kind; his stock of imagery and vacant pictures of the undiscovered bourne are rather soothing, to women particularly, and soft-hearted youths, and can never fail to please, except in the scarce supposable case of a congregation composed entirely of critics.

But then it is all mere sound; your graceful young preacher's prelection has not the least savour of reality. A very different thing is the digging grave and the rugged shovelling Doric of an old sinner like Crawtaes, who has sat out the best part of two generations and seen all his contemporaries laid in the dust. In his peroration the concluding allusion to himself was touching from its homely truth.

" I have had a pretty long life of it, my friends, one way and another—when I look back, I sometimes doubt if I am the same person. When I look back through the storms and drookin mists with which these isles have now become associated in my mind, what a length of time does it seem !

what an effort to the debilitated and all
but forleetit fancy to win back to the day
when I first came among you ! Tongue of
man cannot utter it ! Then the sweet
youth was in love ! And oh ! if it were as
lang a look forward to the day when this
skulking earthly tabernacle shall be dis-
solved, life would seem a wearisome length
indeed. But it is not so. If the morning
of life be too bright for our auld eyes to
look back upon, the evening that is to
close them cometh apace. Yet a little
while—and how short that may be He
only knows in whose hands we all are—
yet a little while, and I too shall be at rest
with him whom we have lost, mine ancient
friend and patron. Amen."

At the conclusion of the service pastor
and laird met in the vestry, where it was
impossible for the latter to avoid shaking

hands with the old man with the friendly
feeling of former days.

A more difficult point to decide was,
whether or not he should ask Mr. Calthrop
to dinner, according to the custom of the
aforesaid gracious days of yore. The
many great objections would probably
have carried it in the negative, had the
day been fine; but it was now far on in
October, and it was blowing and drizzling
in the Frith, the wind contrary, Corbysholm shrouded in fog, the fire across the
way in all probability out, and nothing
cooking; in short, Melethor could not find
it in his heart to let the old man go without his dinner, be the consequences what
they might. He trusted that the restraint
imposed by his father's recent decease
would prevent any very unseemly outbreak on either side. And on this occa-

sion his hospitable trust was not disappointed.

The Lady of Hallow, it is true, was beyond measure astonished and indignant both at her son and the recusant priest when she found herself obliged to receive the latter in the unexpected quality of a Sunday guest; but she was too much a lady to give direct utterance to these feelings. She marked her sense of the old gentleman's short-comings by a reserved yet studious politeness; at which, if the truth must be told, Crawtaes laughed immoderately in his sleeve, quite content to recover his seat at the laird's table on terms so very easy.

But how did friend Logan comport himself in this trying conjuncture? Admirably —with a dignified self-collectedness and command of countenance beyond his years.

Without feeling that he had precisely any title to be either offended or annoyed, he had a pleasing longing that way on finding that he was cutting so small a figure at table compared with the ancient Residuary, who, though coldly looked upon by the lady of the house, kept respectably talking on, and was greatly my friend's over-match in that sort of colloquy: accordingly, Logan restricted his attentions to the number of glasses the old gentleman drank, and other such improving observations.

There is a very good portrait of Crawtaes in a letter of Effie's to her friend Miss Fletcher:

" Yesterday at dinner we met the established minister for the first time. He is a little fat old man and never was married, with the half-merry, half-sad eye of a hard drinker, as Logan tells me he has been all his life. They had very little conversation. It struck me that Mr. Calthrop (which is his rather comical name) was disposed to be on friendly terms, but of course you know it would not have done for Logan to encourage the advances of such a character. The real truth is, I was sorry for the poor old man, who behaved very well upon the whole, though it must be confessed some of his jokes were not altogether right. For instance, on Logan's passing the bottle, he appeared to think this was meant at *him*, and said, ' Ye dinna seem to ken the Latin for guse yet, my young brither—tak a dram if you're wise.' At this I saw the young men smiling to themselves, but fortunately the Master, as they call the eldest, took up the conversation. He is a very clever man, but not so frank as some of the others. Mrs. Deerness kept her temper wonderfully, but we heard that after we were away she had a fit."

END OF VOL. I.

www.ingramcontent.com/pod-product-compliance
Lightning Source LLC
Chambersburg PA
CBHW060551030726
47498CB00005B/1351